S0-AKJ-497

*H*ER strange, elusive beauty had ensnared him as completely as though she were indeed the witch they believed her to be . . . and he knew that even if they were destined to share no more than this brief spell of roving, he would never forget her. Bronwen, the enchantress, the elf-queen. . . .

Also by Sylvia Thorpe:

BEGGAR ON HORSEBACK 23091 $1.50

FAIR SHINE THE DAY 23229 $1.75

A FLASH OF SCARLET 23533 $1.75

THE CHANGING TIDE 23418 $1.75

THE GOLDEN PANTHER 23006 $1.50

THE HIGHWAYMAN 23695 $1.75

THE RELUCTANT ADVENTURESS 23426 $1.50

ROGUE'S COVENANT 23041 $1.50

THE SCANDALOUS LADY ROBIN 23622 $1.75

THE SCAPEGRACE 23478 $1.50

SPRING WILL COME AGAIN 23346 $1.50

THE SWORD AND THE SHADOW 22945 $1.50

SWORD OF VENGEANCE 23136 $1.50

THE VARLEIGH MEDALLION 23900 $1.75

COLUMBIA BOOK SERVICE (a CBS Publications Co.)
32275 Mally Road, P.O. Box FB, Madison Heights, MI 48071

Please send me the books I have checked above. Orders for less than 5 books must include 75¢ for the first book and 25¢ for each additional book to cover postage and handling. Orders for 5 books or more postage is FREE. Send check or money order only.

Cost $_____   Name _____

Postage_____   Address _____

Sales tax*_____ City _____

Total $_____   State _____ Zip _____

* *The government requires us to collect sales tax in all states except AK, DE, MT, NH and OR.*

This offer expires 1/31/81   8999

DARK ENCHANTRESS

Sylvia Thorpe

FAWCETT COVENTRY • NEW YORK

DARK ENCHANTRESS

THIS BOOK CONTAINS THE COMPLETE TEXT OF
THE ORIGINAL HARDCOVER EDITION.

Published by Fawcett Coventry Books, a unit of CBS Publications, the Consumer Publishing Division of CBS Inc., by
arrangement with the Hutchinson Publishing Group, Ltd.

Copyright © 1973 by Sylvia Thorpe

ALL RIGHTS RESERVED

ISBN: 0-449-50052-7

Printed in the United States of America

First Fawcett Coventry printing: June 1980

10   9   8   7   6   5   4   3   2   1

DARK
ENCHANTRESS

Part One

He heard the sound at first faint and far off, so that it encroached upon his consciousness no more than the hum of insects which filled the summer forest, or the spasmodic grumble of the gathering storm. His horse paced slowly along the winding track, for the village which was his immediate destination lay not far ahead, easily to be reached before the storm broke; he meant to lie there that night, continuing his journey on the morrow, and so there was no need to hurry through the sultry, oppressive heat which seemed to press like a tangible thing upon this heavily wooded Essex country-side.

Although it was still early in the evening, there was little light left in the forest. The trees in their heavy summer foliage, and, above them, the clouds hanging slate-grey and purple, combined to create a premature twilight through which horse and rider moved like a ghost, the iron-shod hooves all but soundless on the grassy track. Black horse and black-clad rider. A suit of black velvet lightened only by the broad collar of fine lace; black cloak, scarlet-lined, flung back from wide shoulders; broad-brimmed black hat with a scarlet plume shadowing a swarthy face. A sombre figure in a sombre setting.

The track, which had been gradually climbing, breasted the rise, and the sound of which he had for some time been dimly aware reached him more clearly, so that he reined in and sat listening, eyes narrowed beneath frowning brows, to that confused yet somehow meanacing clamour. Then he urged the horse forward again into a brisk trot, for he had heard that sound before, in other places and at other times, and knew it at once for what it was. The howling of a pack; a human pack, hunting its own kind.

The noise rapidly increased in volume as he advanced, until he could distinguish an occasional word or phrase. "The witch! Kill the witch! To the water with her!" The voices of men and women mingling in one terrifying clamour, and with it the sound of many running feet. The chase was heading towards him, and not far off. He saw that he was approaching the edge of the woods, and drew rein, for he was too experienced a fighter to rush headlong upon unknown odds.

Advancing more cautiously, he saw that the woodland ended abruptly on the brink of a stream, beyond which a stretch of more open country lay revealed in the lurid light of the approaching storm. The track dropped steeply down a short slope to ford the brook and then climbed more gradually to the village a quarter of a mile away, beyond which a column of smoke rose sluggishly into the sultry air. Midway between the stream and the huddle of cottages a mob of men, women and children pounded along the track in pursuit of a woman who fled desperately towards the shelter of the forest.

Halting just within the shadow of the trees he watched them come, the hunters and the hunted. Torn, dishevelled, black hair streaming about her, she ran with that lurching, stumbling gait which tells of endurance almost at an end, of exhausted limbs forced onward only by terror, and by the blind instinct of self-preservation. The foremost pursuers, yelling with triumph, were gaining on her as she reached the brook. She splashed into it, tripped and dropped to her knees in the shallow water, then somehow dragged herself up and stumbled on, up the steep slope beyond. As she reached the top the black horse, obedient to a light touch on the bridle, moved out into the middle of the track.

She halted and stood swaying, staring up out of eyes glazed with fear and hopelessness at the bulk of horse and man looming above her, while the howling mob of her pursuers poured down the further slope. The rider bent forward. She saw an outstretched, black-gloved hand; heard a deep, beautiful, compelling voice say quietly:

"Come, up with you! Give me your hand, then your foot upon mine, and up before me."

Somehow she found the strength to obey, and found herself swung easily up on to the withers of the horse.

9

A sudden, brilliant dazzle of lightning set the beast snorting and rearing with fright, but it was curbed at once by a firm hand and wheeled about and spurred back the way it had come. The shadows of the forest closed about them, and a terrific, rolling clap of thunder drowned the noise of the flying hooves.

The villagers, gripped by superstitious dread, abruptly abandoned the pursuit. The rescue had been too swift and unexpected for them to comprehend. Intent upon their victim, not one of them had noticed the mounted man at the edge of the trees, and it seemed to them that he had materialised without warning out of the darkness of the forest. They had had the barest glimpse of the great black horse and its tall rider, of a swirl of scarlet as their quarry was swept up before him, and then had come that terrible blaze of lightning and crash of thunder to blind and deafen them. By the time they collected their wits the mouth of the track was empty.

Not even the hardiest of them felt inclined to continue the hunt. It was a superstitious age, and before long they had convinced themselves and each other that the horse had had eyes of fire, that the rider had been as tall as the trees and that both had vanished amid the flames of hell. They fled back to their homes, believing that the witch they had hunted had been snatched up, before their awe-stricken eyes, into the embrace of her master, the Devil.

. . . . .

The black horse fled back the way it had come, over the little rise and on into the deepening shadows of the forest until, when half a mile had been covered at an easy canter, its rider drew rein and sat listening for any sound of pursuit. None came, and he turned his attention to the woman he had rescued.

She crouched with hunched shoulders and drooping head in the circle of his supporting arm, one hand pressed to her side as she still fought painfully for breath. Her face was hidden from him by the long black hair which fell all about her, thick and heavy and straight as smoothly flowing water, but already he was realising that the impulse which had prompted him to save her had pitched him into a stranger situation than he had foreseen. A cry of "witch" was not uncommon in country villages in that year of 1653, but usually the victim of it was some aged crone, so poor and senile that she made a convenient scapegoat for her neighbours' misfortunes, and so friendless that no one would lift a hand in her defence. This woman was young, and, from her dress, no village wench. Above the waist her clothing hung in shreds, but her wide shirts were of grass-green silk which, though torn and dusty, and bedraggled where she had stumbled in the stream, still shimmered faintly in the fading light.

"They do not follow," he said at last. "You have no more to fear."

For a moment it seemed that his words made no impression upon her, then slowly she lifted her head and looked about her at the crowding trees, their branches deep-twined above, the bracken standing tall about their trunks; became aware of the forest silence, broken only by the sullen rumbling of the storm; realised that her desperate, hopeless flight had, after all, led to sanctuary. Then, for the first time, she looked up over her shoulder at her rescuer.

In that urgent moment when he swept her up on to his horse he had caught only the most fleeting glimpse of her face, but now, seeing it clearly, he was aware of nothing else in all the world. A strange face, not beautiful, but with some quality about it which made every beautiful face he had ever seen seem insignificant by contrast. A broad, smooth forehead, high cheekbones and a pointed chin; wide, delicately-chiselled mouth; large eyes, of some light colour which in the dimness he could not quite determine, that swept upward at their outer corners beneath slender black brows which followed the same winged line. Into his mind came the memory of an old ballad, heard years before, and long forgotten, about the "queen of elf-land", for this was a face which seemed to belong to a realm remote from the commonplace world of every day.

Lightning flickered again above the trees and, piercing the dusk beneath, brought him abruptly back to the reality of the present moment. Tearing his gaze away from the girl's face, he looked frowningly about him.

"This is no place to be during a thunderstorm. Is there any shelter nearby that we may safely seek?"

"I know of only one place." Her voice was faint, still broken and ragged with her uneven breathing, but it was the voice of a gentlewoman. "Ride on a little. I will show you the way."

He did so, and after a minute or two she pointed out a narrower track leading off to the right, which in turn gave place to a path so narrow that fronds of bracken brushed the horse's flanks. So they rode on, deep and

12

ever deeper into the forest, until he knew he could never retrace their steps unaided. The path dwindled and vanished, they were forcing their way through a sea of tangled bracken, and now it was the woman who guided the horse, one white hand light upon the bridle. They rode in silence, while lightning flickered constantly through the branches and the grumbling voice of the storm rolled nearer, until suddenly he realised that there were remains of ruined buildings among the trees, fragments of wall so smothered in moss and ivy that at first glance they seemed a natural part of the woodland. Then they were in a small clearing where a stream slid tinkling over a stony bed, and a larger, less completely ruined building loomed beyond.

"There is shelter of a sort," she said in a low voice, "and safety, for no one comes here."

She let the horse splash through the stream, and then drew rein and slid lightly to the ground. He dismounted and followed her through a crumbling archway into what seemed to be the remains of a small church, with broken pillars and, here and there, a scrap of carving, or of window tracery which had once framed stained glass. Part of the roof had fallen to lie in piles of tumbled masonry on the worn flagstones, but enough remained at one corner to provide shelter for them and their mount.

"It will serve," he said laconically. "Bide here while I tend the horse."

He went out again and took the beast to the stream to drink, and then led it within, unsaddled it, and tethered it to one of the pillars. For a while he paid no heed to his companion, but when his task was done he found that she had gone to the furthest corner of the ruin, where dead leaves had drifted into a pile in an angle of the ancient walls, and was sitting on this meagre couch with her arms clasped about her knees and her head bowed upon them. As he laid the saddle down nearby, she spoke without looking up.

"Why did you help me? Did you not hear the cry of 'witch' as they hunted me?"

"I heard it!" He sounded contemptuous. "I have yet to learn, though, that a thing must be truth merely because it is howled by an ignorant rabble."

She still did not move. "What if it were true? Have you no fears for your immortal soul?"

He laughed, seating himself on a nearby block of stone. "Those godly folk who name you witch would say that my soul is already damned beyond all hope of salvation. Why, then, should I be fearful?"

Now at last she lifted her head to stare at him, her face pale between the black, gleaming curtains of her hair. Her voice was low, almost fearful, as she asked: "Who are you?"

He shrugged. "A stranger, passing this way by chance. My name is Benedict Forde. And you?"

"I am called Bronwen."

It had begun to rain, large drops pattering noisily on the leaves and rapidly increasing to a downpour. It cascaded through the broken roof and bounced in little spurts from the stone floor, a silvery curtain shutting off the sheltered corner where they sat. Lightning crackled, bathing the scene for a fraction of a second in eerie brilliance, and a long roll of thunder echoed round the crumbling walls.

"Bronwen," Benedict Forde repeated thoughtfully. "No more than that?"

"It is the name bestowed on me at my birth," she replied sullenly. "If I have a right to any other, I know nothing of it."

"A foundling?" There was disbelief in his voice. "A foundling who goes clad in silk, and speaks in the accents of a gentlewoman?"

"I was gently reared—my foster-father was Sir Edwin Aldon of Twyning Hall—but I am a foundling none the less."

"He *was* your foster-father?"

Bronwen's head went down again upon her arms; her next words were muffled. "He died a twelvemonth since."

For a space there was silence, broken only by the rush and hiss of the falling rain. Benedict leaned back against the wall and contemplated his companion's bowed figure, the stained and crumpled skirts, the black hair spread like a cloak across white arms and shoulders. He wanted her to look up; wanted to see again that strangely fascinating face with the mysterious eyes.

"And now you flee for your life from a mob that names you witch," he remarked. "How come you to such a pass? Did your foster-father leave you unprotected and unprovided for?"

"He made provision—generously," Bronwen said bitterly. She raised her head, as he had hoped she would, but instead of looking at him, sat staring straight before her. "But his Will was set aside by the courts at the plea of kinfolk greedy to inherit everything that was his, and I driven forth from the only home I had ever known." She paused, hunching her shoulders in a gesture both weary and petulant. "What use to speak of it? They have taken all, and today would have had my life, too, but for your aid."

"Perhaps I can aid you yet further. Tell me more of these rogues who have stolen your inheritance."

"Rogues?" she repeated. "Why, so they are, but in the guise of honest men, and with the weight of the law behind them. Neither you nor anyone can aid me against such as they."

"How can either of us be sure of that unless you tell me the whole story?"

"*I* am sure," she said sullenly. "They stand secure, and even if they did not I would never dare to challenge them now. Do you not know that to be named witch is to be condemned to death, either hounded by the mob or sentenced by due process of the law? The Aldons hoped I would be killed today, but even though you prevented that, I can never again be any danger to them."

"As to that, we shall see. Tell me how they raised that rabble against you." She made no reply, and after a moment he repeated, very gently: "Tell me, Bronwen."

Slowly, as though against her will, she turned her head to look at him. Benedict Forde was by no means a handsome man. His face, shaven like a Puritan's although his dark hair fell curling over his shoulders, was lean to the point of gauntness and as swarthy as a gypsy's, with dark eyes deep-set beneath heavy brows, and a slightly crooked nose. Deep lines were scored

16

from nose to mouth, and though the mouth itself showed humour, this was of a sardonic kind, suggesting a faintly contemptuous tolerance of the world and his fellow men. A forbidding face, but his looks seemed unimportant as soon as he spoke, for his voice was sheer magic, deep and resonant and marvellously expressive, making poetry and music of the simplest words.

Bronwen had been conscious of the power of that voice even when, almost fainting with terror and exhaustion, she had been scarcely aware of the man himself. She was conscious of it now. Beneath its spell, she began to speak; to tell this man, this stranger to whom she owed her life, all that had happened during the past few months. Months which had reduced her from her position as the mistress of Twyning Hall to a hunted outcast whose very life was forfeit.

Part Two

Bronwen, released by a servant from the bedchamber in which she had been imprisoned for the past three days, went slowly down the stairs at Twyning Hall, summoned by the new master of the house, Sir John Aldon. She walked slowly because she was still stiff and sore from the whipping which had been another part of her punishment, but she appeared in no way chastened by her humiliations. She seemed, in fact, to have acquired added dignity from them.

So it seemed, at least, to the thin, pale-faced youth who watched her from a nearby doorway, and who came quickly, if somewhat furtively, to meet her. Francis Aldon, the younger of Sir John's two sons.

"Bronwen," he said in a low, urgent voice, "how is it with you?"

She shrugged, pausing on the lowest stair with one

hand on the heavily carved newel-post. "How is it with anyone who has been soundly beaten and kept for three days on a diet of bread and water?"

"I know! I know!" he agreed wretchedly. "But you angered my father so greatly, Bronwen, and—and you have fared no worse than we have all done at sometime or another, I and my brother and sisters."

"Then no doubt you and your brother and sisters are accustomed to it. I am not."

He looked honestly surprised. "Did Sir Edwin never chastise you, then?"

"Not by whipping and imprisonment," she replied scornfully, "but Sir Edwin was a wise and a just man, not an ignorant, narrow-minded bigot."

"Bronwen!" Francis cast an anxious, hurried glance over his shoulder. "Have a care what you say. Suppose anyone but I had heard those words?"

"Then it would have been a very short space of time before Sir John heard them in his turn," she retorted in the same contemptuous tone. "How eager you all are to curry favour with him by carrying tales of one another! Why do *you* not hasten to him, Francis, and tell him that I am no more afraid to speak the truth about him now than I was when he burned Sir Edwin's books?"

"If I did my duty, I *would* tell him what you have said," Francis said miserably, "but that would only bring further punishment upon you. I could never forgive myself for that."

She cast him a swift, unreadable glance beneath her lashes. "Will your conscience allow you to forgive yourself for *not* doing what you call your duty?"

"It would not let me rest if I deliberately caused you more suffering," he assured her earnestly, and ventured to lay his hand over hers where it still rested on the newel-post. "To beat you so cruelly! Oh, Bronwen, I cannot bear to think of it!"

"Then do not," she said coolly. "It can profit neither of us."

"I cannot help myself," he said in a stifled voice. "You are never out of my thoughts."

He bent his head and pressed an awkward kiss on to her wrist. She did not move, but stood looking down with some scorn at the bowed fair head, for she had been aware from the first of his infatuation and found it mildly irritating. Francis was seventeen, only three years younger than Bronwen herself, but to her he seemed no more than a schoolboy. He stood very much in awe of his father, and since Bronwen's bitter resentment towards Sir John was still, in spite of the pain and indignity she had suffered at his hands, utterly untainted by fear, this roused her impatience rather than her compassion.

"Then you would do well to dissemble those thoughts," she said indifferently. "We should both suffer if your father suspected them—and the direction they have been taking." His head jerked up, and a dull flush suffused his face as he met the mockery in her eyes. "Oh yes, *I* know it! A woman does not find such thoughts hard to read."

She withdrew her hand from his slackened clasp, and without another word went past him and across the hall towards the library. Francis stood staring after her, his face hot with embarrassment, not realising that he had passed from her mind the moment he had passed from her sight.

In the library, Sir John had taken up a commanding position before the fireplace, his back to the empty hearth. He was a small man, and truculent as small men often are; his present attitude showed it. He stood with feet wide planted, hands clasped behind him and his chin, with its fair, greying beard, aggressively out-thrust. In a high-backed chair a few paces away sat his wife, a lady whose proportions were as ample as his were sparse. She had taken a dislike to Bronwen as soon as she saw her, and did not trouble to conceal it.

In silence they watched the girl enter the room, cross it towards them, drop the smallest formal curtsy that politeness demanded, then stand before them with folded hands. Bronwen was aware of their hostility even though she kept her eyes lowered. It reached out to her, almost tangible.

"So, mistress," Sir John said at length, "you have had three days of solitude in which to reflect and re-pent. I trust you have profited from them."

"Repent of what, Sir John?" Her voice was quiet and she did not raise her eyes, but her tone bit. "I have only one regret. That I did not succeed in preventing an act of wanton, wicked destruction."

"I see you have *not* profited from the lesson," he said angrily. "Must I whip you again to impress upon you that you have no right to criticise what I may or may not do, and to teach you a proper respect for my authority?"

Very slowly Bronwen raised her eyes and looked full into his, for he and she were much the same height; if anything, she was a fraction taller. "You may whip the skin from my back," she said deliberately, "and the breath from my body, but I will never respect you. No, nor fear you, either."

Lady Aldon uttered an exclamation which expressed in one comprehensive sound shock, indignation and expectancy—the expectancy of seeing this insolent wench crushed by Sir John's just anger. Sir John, however, disappointed his lady, although his face darkened with fury. The truth was that everything about Bronwen made him feel uncomfortable, but nothing more so than her eyes, with their strange, upward slant and even stranger colour. Grey eyes, he had thought the first time he saw her, but then he had realised that they were not grey, but green. The clear, cold green of seawater. There was something uncanny about them, and now, before their contemptuous gaze, he felt at a distinct disadvantage.

"I have no wish to be feared," he said at last, "but I *will* be respected by all who dwell beneath my roof. Yes, and obeyed by them also. This house is mine now, and I will harbour within it none of the evil which my misguided kinsman had seen fit to amass. Books in heathenish tongues, mystical charts and drawings—such things are the tools of the Devil."

"The drawings and charts were astrological, as you would have known if you had even the smallest degree of learning," she replied impatiently. "The books recorded the thoughts and discoveries of wise men in other lands and other days. Sir Edwin spent his life in a quest for the truth."

"Truth is to be found only in Holy Writ. To seek it

elsewhere is to traffic with the Devil. The abomination of evil which I found in this room was dealt with as it deserved when I consigned it to the flames."

Bronwen looked about her; at the empty shelves which until three days ago had housed Sir Edwin's priceless collection of books; at the table where she had so often sat with him to study. While this room remained unchanged it was as though her foster-father had not entirely left her. Now there was only emptiness and desolation.

"The wisdom of ages," she said bitterly, "and the work of a lifetime in gathering it together. And you in your ignorance burned it all—without even the right to do so. The books were mine. Sir Edwin willed them to me."

"The courts have judged the question of Sir Edwin's Will," Sir John reminded her, "and they found in my favour, so do not have the impudence to prate to me of rights. You have none whatsoever."

"Nor ever had," Lady Aldon put in spitefully. "The nameless brat of a wanton mother who would have starved but for Sir Edwin's misguided charity. Yet you flaunt yourself in silken gowns as though you were a lady born."

Bronwen glanced at her with cool comprehension, indifferent to a gibe which she knew the other woman had been unable to resist. Sir John, as much from meanness as from religious or political convictions, kept his family very plainly clad, but Sir Edwin had liked to see his foster-daughter finely dressed, and since emerging from the nursery Bronwen had never worn anything but silks and satins. It had therefore seemed natural to choose the same rich materials for her mourning-clothes, but she had soon realised that Lady Aldon and her daughters and daughter-in-law resented seeing her in gowns such as the one she now wore, of stiff black silk trimmed with black velvet and a broad collar of costly lace.

"Perhaps, madam, I *am* a lady born," she said mockingly. "Alas, we shall never know!"

"Enough!" Sir John said angrily. "Such talk is unseemly. I repeat, Mistress Bronwen, that you have no rights whatsoever, but, since my kinsman made himself responsible for you, I shall not shirk the duty which has been thrust upon me. You may remain at Twyning Hall as a member of my household, but remember! You will obey me in all things."

"And if I do not?"

"You have already had one taste of the results of disobedience and defiance. Take warning from it, for I shall be less lenient another time. And one thing more! I do not intend to support you in idleness. You will take your share of household tasks, performing whatever duties her ladyship sees fit to allot to you."

Bronwen, glancing at Lady Aldon, saw malicious triumph in her face and knew that she could look for no mercy there. She would be reduced to the status of a servant. She, who had been mistress of the house. That was a humiliation she could not, would not face.

"You are frank, Sir John," she said quietly, "so now, I pray, answer me one question with equal frankness. What if I were to tell you I will not stay?"

She thought she saw the merest hint of a triumphant smile touch the bearded lips, but it was gone in a flash and she could not even be sure that it had been there at all.

"It is seldom, mistress, that our inclinations go hand-in-hand with our needs," he said pompously, "but you need not fear that I shall constrain you. While you remain in my house I have authority over you, but I cannot compel you to remain in it. That choice must be yours. I will say only this—that as long as I am master of Twyning Hall there will be a place for you beneath its roof. Think well before . . ."

He paused, checked in mid-sentence by a sudden, over-whelming sense of disquiet. Bronwen was still looking at him—that is, her gaze was still turned towards him—but he knew with chilling certainty that she saw him no longer. Her eyes had dilated a little; she seemed to be looking through and beyond him as though he, his wife and the room they occupied had ceased to exist, and he knew himself to be in the presence of something he could not comprehend. So for a few, heart-stopping seconds, and then the rapt look faded from her face; she came back, as it were, to the reality of place and time; but now there was a new expression in her eyes as she looked at him. The expression with which a judge might regard a prisoner newly sentenced, or a physician a sick man for whom he knew no cure.

"Master of Twyning Hall," she repeated quietly. "Yes, for a space, since by cunning you have made yourself so, but your triumph will not endure. It will be as ashes, and the name of Aldon perish and be known no more."

Sir John's face was ashen, his truculence completely

gone; Lady Aldon shrank back in her chair. For a few seconds longer Bronwen stood there, regarding them both with a look almost of pity in her eyes, and then she turned and went out. Neither of them made any attempt to stop her.

She encountered no one as she returned to her bedchamber. Calmly, methodically, she gathered together certain of her possessions; clothing, trinkets, her little store of money. She made them into as small and compact a bundle as she could contrive, cast a cloak about her shoulders, and taking up her burden, went downstairs again, across the hall and out through the great oak door into the cool, still beauty of the spring evening. She saw no one, spoke to no one; and so, with no word of farewell and without a backward glance, Bronwen departed from the only home she had ever known.

•　　•　　•　　•　　•

She took refuge in a tumbledown, deserted cottage on the outskirts of the village of Twyning Green, a scant half-mile from the Hall. It had once been part of the Aldon estate, but at some time, for reasons long forgotten, it had passed, with the patch of land on which it stood, into the possession of the family who dwelt in it. The last survivor of that family, an old woman of solitary disposition and evil temper, had fallen victim to the upsurge of witch-mania which had swept through the county eight years before, inspired by the infamous Matthew Hopkins, self-styled Witchfinder-General. Someone in the village had cried "witch", the crone had been seized and dragged off to prison and, in spite of

26

the efforts of Sir Edwin to save her, tried and convicted. Since then the cottage had stood empty, falling slowly into ruin. Remembrance of the witch still lingered about it and the villagers gave it a wide berth, but to Bronwen it offered a providential answer to the urgent problem of finding shelter. She dare not waste such money as she had by lodging at the inn, nor did she relish the curiosity and speculation which would surround her there.

In the lengthening shadows of evening the cottage, with its sagging roof and broken shutters, and the tangle of weeds and briars which grew to the very threshold, was a dreary sight, but it was at least better than spending the night under a hedgerow. Bronwen did not fear the reputation of the place. Sir Edwin had scorned the idea that old Abby had been a witch, and it never occurred to Bronwen to doubt his judgment.

She had had the forethought to include a tinder-box and candles in her bundle, but since she had brought no food was obliged to go supperless to bed—the latter a heap of young branches and bracken which she gathered by the last of the daylight, and on which she slept wrapped in her cloak and with the bundle of clothing for a pillow.

Next day young Francis came seeking her, and found her doing what she could to make the cottage's single room more habitable. It was still meagerly furnished, for the villagers had been afraid to steal anything that had belonged to the witch, and since the sturdy table, stools and bed-frame were all of rough-hewn oak, they had survived the years of neglect, as had the iron cooking-pots which hung above the hearth. Bronwen, with her satin skirts caught up and an apron to protect her petticoats, was wielding a broom she had fashioned out of a bundle of twigs tied to a stick, but paused when Francis's shadow darkened the low-pitched doorway. He looked about him in horror, from the bare earthen floor below to the bare, smoke-blackened rafters above.

"Bronwen, you cannot stay in this filthy hovel!"

"I stayed in it last night and came to no harm," she replied calmly, "and it will not be filthy when I have done. Why are you here, Francis?"

"Did you think you could walk out of the house and no attempt be made to find you? I was nearly demented with anxiety when I learned you had gone. I have been seeking you since daybreak, but at first I went farther afield, for I never supposed you would linger in the village. I thought you would seek shelter with friends."

Brownwen shrugged. "I have none."

"But Sir Edwin, surely, was on terms of friendship with the other gentry hereabouts?"

"Sir Edwin, my dear Francis, had neither the leisure nor the inclination for such trivial matters. In his youth, as you may know, he spent many years travelling abroad in quest of learning, while within my own memory he devoted himself entirely to the further pursuit of knowledge, and scarcely left the house."

Francis was staring at her. "You have led a strange and lonely life, have you not?"

"Strange, perhaps, but not lonely. I was content to be Sir Edwin's pupil. To study, to learn." Abruptly she changed the subject. "Does Sir John know you are here?"

"He knows that I came seeking you. He bade me remind you, if I found you, that there is still a home for you at the Hall."

"To be sure," she agreed mockingly. "As waiting-woman to your mother, your sisters and your brother's wife. Sir John already knows my answer to that. He knew what it would be even before he told me upon what conditions I would be permitted to stay." She laughed shortly. "Your father, Francis, is a hypocrite. I am an embarrassment of which he wishes to rid himself, but since his kinsman treated me as a daughter he cannot well turn me out of doors. So he makes it impossible for me to stay, and then declares that I refused his generosity and left of my own free will. Thus he cannot be held to blame for any mischance which may befall me."

"You misjudge him, Bronwen," Francis assured her earnestly. "When he told us last night of your departure he confessed to deep misgiving on your behalf. And he is right! It is not seemly, it is not even safe for a young woman to live alone and unprotected."

"No one will trouble me here," she said indifferently. "The villagers shun this as a place accursed."

"I do not wonder at it!" Francis looked uneasily about him. "Do you not fear to stay here?"

"No, why should I? Even if the poor hag who dwelt here *was* a witch, she was hanged eight years ago. Besides, I do not think she would grudge me the shelter of her roof."

"Then you will not come home?"

"I have no home," she replied bitterly, "save such as

I may make here. But do you go, Francis, for I can see that you are not easy in this place."

"I *will* go, but I shall return before dark." He caught her hand in both of his and kissed it fervently. "Before dark!" he repeated, and hurried away.

Bronwen followed him to the door and stood there, leaning on her makeshift broom, to watch him ride away. Then she shrugged, and returned to the task of rendering the cottage as habitable as possible with the meagre resources at her disposal.

Later, when she went out to gather wood for her fire, she saw a group of children watching her from a safe distance, but this did not greatly surprise her. That morning, when she had gone into the village to buy food from the cottagers, she had been aware of stares and whispers following her, and guessed that the tale of her departure from the Hall was already common knowledge. No doubt, when the novelty of her presence had worn off, they would accept her.

She scarcely expected to see Francis again that day, but towards sunset he returned, this time leading a laden pack-horse. While Bronwen watched in astonishment he unloaded the beast, carrying into the cottage bedding, cooking utensils, pewter plates and mugs and an ample store of food. Conquering her amazement, she tried to stop him.

"Are these things an offering to ease your father's conscience, Francis, or did you fetch them from the Hall without his knowledge? In either event, I want none of them."

"Yet you need them all. I did not bring them from the Hall, Bronwen. I rode to Epping and purchased

30

them there." He put down the articles he was carrying and faced her belligerently. "If you are determined on this madness, at least let me make some provision for you."

"I do not look for charity."

"Nor do I offer it. I bring you a gift, for—for friendship's sake." He stared at her, half truculent, half pleading. "Can you not accept it, for the same reason?"

For a moment she continued to frown at him, then her expression softened and she smiled.

"I am churlish and ungrateful," she said remorsefully. "Forgive me, Francis. I accept your gift, and that most thankfully."

She put out her hand to him as she spoke and he took it eagerly, but when he tried to draw her into his arms she freed herself, gently but firmly.

"For friendship's sake, Francis," she reminded him. "No more than that."

·   ·   ·   ·   ·   ·

In the weeks which followed she continued to hold him at arm's length, though this grew increasingly difficult. She even did her best to discourage him from visiting the cottage at all, in spite of the loneliness which she found so hard to endure. The villagers, at a loss to know how to treat one whom they had been used to regard as the daughter of the manor but who now lived as humbly as they did themselves, avoided her. At times she would see them, children and even the occasional adult, staring at the cottage from beyond the weed-grown wilderness of the garden, but they never

31

replied to her greetings, and even when she went to procure food, trailing her silken skirts incongruously along the dusty street, they spoke to her no more than necessity demanded. Rebuffed in this fashion, and too proud to try to overcome the barrier, she took refuge in an aloofness which did nothing to endear her to them.

Deprived of human companionship, she turned instead to the small wild creatures of the countryside, and it was not long before birds would come fluttering about her as soon as she stepped outside the house, eager for the scraps of food she scattered, and one of them, a robin, would even feed from her hand. Then one day she found a baby rabbit lying injured, and carried it home and tended it, until it became so tame that it would follow her about like a pet dog, and allow her to pick it up and fondle it whenever she wished.

Hers was a hard life now by comparison with the plenty she had always known, and though she knew she was less unhappy than she would have been under the changed conditions at Twyning Hall, there was a nagging worry at the back of her mind, a certainty that her present situation could not be indefinitely prolonged. This was confirmed by something which Francis said to her one day. He had never ceased to urge her to return to the Hall, and finally, vexed by her persistent refusal, he said angrily:

"That is all very fine while summer lasts, but it will be a different tale when winter comes. You will be obliged to come back then, as my father has said all along."

Bronwen stared at him, understanding suddenly

several things which had been puzzling her. Sir John had allowed her to leave his house even though it was an unheard-of thing for a young, unmarried woman, gently reared, to fend for herself; he had made no protest when she provoked gossip by settling in a ruinous cottage almost at his gates; he had even permitted his younger son to visit her and to provide her with various necessities. She had thought this strange, but now she perceived that he was more subtle than she had supposed. Convinced that the onset of winter would drive her back to the Hall, he was content to bide his time; to be ready with the magnanimous gesture, the generous forgiving of her troublesome prank. The fault would appear to be all on her side. Sir John would figure in the eyes of gentle and simple alike as a kindly, tolerant man—and she would have placed herself completely at his mercy.

"Summer or winter, I bide here," she said defiantly. "You may tell Sir John that, if you choose."

The words were bold, but when Francis had ridden away, still in an ill humour, she forced herself to face the truth, and to admit that she was unlikely to be able to make good her boast. The cottage would be uninhabitable in winter. Even now, draughts whistled between the broken shutters and rain found its way through the roof. She would lack the means to purchase either food or fuel, for her little store of money was diminishing at an alarming rate, and though Francis would no doubt be willing to supply her needs, she could not accept his generosity with one hand, and continue to rebuff his increasingly amorous advances with the other. The only alternative, apart from a re-

33

turn to the Hall, would be to leave the village altogether for one of the larger towns, and she had no illusions regarding what that would mean. There was only one way in which a woman in her situation could earn a living.

Yet, while summer lasted, she was determined not to give way, whatever bitter choice might be forced upon her when winter came. Her greatest enemy was loneliness. She had lived all her life in a large household, and for nearly five years had been mistress of it, but now for days at a time she never spoke to another human being.

There had been an indefinable change in the attitude of the villagers, and where at first their reluctance to accept her had been prompted by embarrassment, she now sensed a resentment which, strangely, seemed tinged with fear. They still supplied her modest needs, but in a way which suggested that, though they dare not refuse, they would very much prefer to have no dealings with her at all. Children still came and stood in staring, whispering groups beyond the boundaries of her garden—in fact, it seemed to Bronwen that they came more often and in increasing numbers—but the moment she stepped from the house, or if she encountered them elsewhere, they took to their heels.

Once more it was Francis who provided a clue to the mystery, when she met him one day on her way home after a morning spent gathering berries and herbs to eke out her frugal meals. He overtook her a short way from the cottage, and she greeted him with more warmth than she usually showed, simply because it was such a relief to see a friendly face.

He dismounted, eyeing her with admiration, for instead of the black in which he had always previously seen her, she was wearing a gown of grass-green silk, its bodice cut wide and low and trimmed with a narrow edging of fine lace. The green reflected and deepened the colour of her eyes, and flattered the contrast between her night-black hair and the milky whiteness of her skin, which not even the summer sun had succeeded in tingeing with gold.

"You have put off your mourning," he said. "How beautiful you look."

"I have put it off for a very practical reason," she replied dampingly. "A pedlar I knew came by yesterday, and since my money was almost gone, I sold him my trinkets and my other gowns. This one he would not take, for he said no one would buy a grass-green gown. It is the fairy colour, and therefore unlucky." She made a wry grimace. "Perhaps he is right. I wore this for the first time only two days before Sir Edwin died, and it is certain I have had little good luck since."

"Why did you not tell me that you were so hardpressed?" he demanded. "I would have aided you."

She shook her head. "I will not take money from you, Francis. You brought me a gift and I was grateful for it, but that was both the beginning, and the end."

"You could have taken the money as a loan. I would even have held your trinkets as surety if it would have eased your mind."

"How could I accept a loan when there is not the smallest prospect of ever being able to repay it? That

35

would have been more contemptible than taking money outright."

"Bronwen," he said urgently, "this cannot go on! You *must* come back to the Hall. Whatever sum the pedlar paid you will not last for ever, and then what will you do?"

They were walking on along the lane, Francis leading his horse. Bronwen did not reply at once.

"I do not know," she said at length, "save that I will not come crawling to your father to beg as charity that which is mine by right."

"You may have no choice," he said soberly. "We had word today that my uncle, Colonel Giles Aldon, is coming here."

"Your father's younger brother? What is that to me?"

"It may be much." Francis's tone was grave. "He knows what has happened, and says that it is not to be tolerated. If his brother, he says, allows himself to be mocked at and defied by an impudent foundling wench—forgive me, Bronwen, but it was thus he wrote to my father—*he* will not, and since it seems that no one here can bring you to a proper sense of shame, he will do so himself."

"Will he, indeed?" There was an edge to Bronwen's voice. "I suppose a poor foundling should be honoured that so important a man should concern himself over her."

"Do not mock at him. He *is* an important man, greatly trusted by General Cromwell, and high in his favour. And he will be more important yet. He is ambitious for our family. It was he who urged my father to challenge Sir Edwin's Will."

"I begin to understand," she said scornfully. "Since Sir Edwin cared only for learning and declared neither for King nor Parliament during the late wars, his fortune remains intact, a rich prize for anyone strong enough and unscrupulous enough to take it. Like your uncle."

"The courts found in my father's favour."

"Of course! *I* have no powerful friends in London. The only thing which astonishes me is that Colonel Aldon considers me important enough to merit his notice."

"He will not brook defiance," Francis explained. "Not from anyone. Perhaps, too, he fears it may become known that you, whom Sir Edwin reared as his daughter, are living in poverty not half a mile from the Hall. It would not look well. Our family—and especially my uncle—have enemies. It is always so when one rises swiftly to wealth and honours."

"Especially when one does not care what means one uses to achieve such eminence. Let Colonel Aldon come. I would not return at your father's bidding, and still less will I return at his."

"Then return at mine! No, not at my bidding, but because I beg you to do so. You think my father a harsh man, but, believe me, he is mildness itself compared with his brother. If you are back home by the time he comes, if you admit your fault and show a proper repentance, you may not fare too badly. If you do not, there is no telling what the end may be."

"Why, what can he do? I tell you, Francis, if

Colonel Aldon wants me at the Hall, he will need to drag me back by force, and to keep me under lock and key when he has me there."

"Even that would not surprise me, but, Bronwen, there is another reason why you must return." He hesitated, and then added miserably: "I did not want to tell you, but for your own sake I must. There are rumours abroad in the village."

"Rumours?" Bronwen stared at him. "Rumours of what?"

"About Sir Edwin. Did you not tell me that he was a solitary man who deliberately cut himself off from all dealings with his neighbours?"

"There are none among them of sufficient learning. He preferred the company of his books."

"Yet you were his close and constant companion, and no one else was allowed even to touch those books?"

"I was his pupil. As for the books, they were beyond price and he trusted no one else to use them as they deserved."

"Yet as soon as my father had examined them, he ordered them to be burned, and you behaved like one demented, trying to prevent it. The villagers have heard of this from the servants, who have also told, those who carried the books out to the fire, how some of these contained strange characters unlike to Christian letters, and mystical charts and drawings. Now they begin to whisper"—Francis glanced uneasily about him and lowered his voice a little—"that Sir Edwin sought to traffic with the Devil."

"Fools!" Bronwen spoke with angry contempt. "Ignorant, superstitious fools!"

"Mayhap they are, but such whispers can be dangerous. These people have also seen you leave the Hall to take up your abode in the abandoned home of a proven witch. Bronwen, do you not realise that peril may threaten you?"

She forced herself to consider the matter dispassionately, without the anger which had been her first, involuntary reaction. In the light of what Francis had told her, the fear and hostility she had sensed among the villagers, and the staring children who fled at her approach, took on an ominous significance.

"So you see," he was saying earnestly, "you must come back. For your own sake, your own safety. Once you are again accepted in my father's house, these evil rumours will die. You must see the wisdom of that!"

"Or of removing altogether from this place," she added, half to herself. They had reached the cottage now, and she stood looking at the cheerless, tumbledown little house crouching beneath the trees which almost surrounded it, cutting it off from the rest of the village. "I would not be sorry to go."

"Would you not? Would you not indeed?" Francis had paused also, but after one cursory glance at the cottage, fixed his eager gaze on Bronwen's face. "Bronwen, listen to me! In a week's time I shall be eighteen, and from the day I attain that age I shall have money of my own, a legacy from my godfather. I will take you away! I'll find you a decent lodging in Epping—under an assumed name, if need be—where you can be safe and comfortable, and not put to such shifts as selling your gowns and trinkets to buy food. Oh, Bronwen, tell me that you will come!"

While he spoke she had turned from contemplation of the cottage to contemplation of him; of the thin, rather weak young face, now flushed and eager; of the unsteadiness of the hand he stretched out to clasp hers. She let it lie unresponsive in his. Her wide, green, slanted eyes held an unreadable expression.

"And if I do," she said quietly, "what will you want in return?"

"You know what I want," he replied in a low voice. "I want *you*! I have loved you from the moment I met you. I think you have bewitched me, for, waking or sleeping, I think of nothing else."

Still she watched him with that unfathomable gaze. "And will you marry me, Francis?"

"Marry you?" There was sharp dismay in his voice. "I cannot! You must know that I cannot. My father would never give his consent."

"But he would consent to you taking me as your mistress?"

"That is a different matter," he said quickly, and added ingenuously: "Besides, he need never know."

"I think you underestimate him," Bronwen replied, and now there was a faint edge of scorn, like frost-crystals, to her voice. "How long do you think you could keep such a secret? And what of me? Am I to be hidden away in some discreet corner to wait humbly until you find it convenient to visit me?"

"Do you think that is what *I* want?" he said wretchedly. "The world could hold no greater happiness for me than to have you always at my side, but it is not possible. There is another reason for my uncle's visit. He is coming to discuss the question of my marriage. A bride has already been chosen for me."

"And you will submit to this without protest?"

"How can I do otherwise? Her father is a man of wealth and great influence whom my uncle is anxious to attach to our interests. He—my uncle—has no son, and so he has suggested the young lady to my father as a suitable match for me, and my father has agreed. You have been reared as an Aldon, Bronwen! You know how important prudent marriages are to families such as ours."

Bronwen looked at him, and suddenly all her hatred of his family, all her resentment of the wrongs they had done her, rose up with a force which could not be denied. Her glance raked him contemptuously from head to foot; her voice cut like a blade of tempered steel.

"I was reared as the foster-child of a wise and kindly man, but not as an Aldon. No, never that! I will not be accounted part of a family which sets bigotry above learning, greed above common justice, and ambition above everything. I wish your bride joy of the union, Francis, but know this! You could not buy your way into *my* bed even at the price of a marriage-ring."

With a disdainful swirl of her silken skirts she turned towards the cottage, but Francis let fall the bridle of his horse and sprang after her, gripping her by the arm. With a violence for which she was unprepared he swung her round again to face him.

"Do you flatter yourself that such a price would ever have been offered?" The flush had faded from his face,

41

leaving it livid; his voice shook uncontrollably. "You are too proud, my girl, for a homeless, penniless foundling! It's time you were humbled!"

He caught her against him and thrust her down against the steep, crumbling bank which formed the boundary of the cottage garden, holding her with one arm and the weight of his body while he rained clumsy kisses on her face and throat, and his free hand fumbled at the bodice of her gown. But he was not strong enough to maintain his mastery over the writhing, kicking, clawing fury she had become, and after a few moments she succeeded in thrusting him away. His heel caught in a rut and he measured his length on the ground, while she, coming to her feet in one swift, lithe movement, looked down at him with eyes blazing as green as those of an angry cat.

"But not by you!" Her voice was cold and clear, icy with disdain. "When I take a lover it will be of my own free will, and he a man, not a weak-willed boy hag-ridden by an ambitious family. And a man, Francis, you will never be!"

A movement on the far side of the lane caught her eye and she looked quickly in that direction, to see two village children, a boy and a girl of about twelve years of age, peering open-mouthed from among the bushes there. Finding themselves discovered, they took to their heels, racing away towards the centre of the village, while Bronwen, ignoring Francis who had now scrambled to his feet, swept through her weed-grown garden and into the cottage.

Francis hesitated, as though debating whether or not to follow her, and then with a muttered imprecation he retrieved his hat, clapped it on his head, mounted his horse, and rode furiously away in the direction of Twyning Hall.

.   .   .   .   .

Bronwen sat in the cottage and combed her hair. Usually she found it soothing, the long, steady sweep of the comb through the heavy tresses that fell to below her waist, but this evening the customary restful effect was lacking. She felt tense and on edge, and a sense of oppression weighed upon her.

Although it still lacked some hours to nightfall, it was almost dark in the little, low-pitched room where the embers on the hearth glowed dull and baleful. The door stood wide, for the air was heavy and sultry with a threatening storm and such light as remained was lurid, a sinister, yellowish glow trapped beneath low, slate-blue and purple clouds. Now and then lightning flickered, and thunder muttered in the distance.

Bronwen was thinking of what Francis had told her the day before; she had thought of little else ever since. Her anger against the villagers had subsided, for one could not blame ignorant country folk for superstitions which were shared even by a supposedly educated man like Sir John Aldon, but she knew that Francis had exaggerated her danger. Probably suspicion of Sir Edwin's activities had festered beneath the surface even during his lifetime, and now events since the arrival of Sir John had brought it out into the open; and, if she knew anything at all of village life, it had lost nothing in the telling.

It was obvious that she must leave the neighbourhood of Twyning Hall, and she was wondering now if she had been foolish and improvident to repulse Francis as she had done. Would it have been so great a matter to yield to his entreaties? She desperately needed help, and he was sufficiently devoted to her to give it generously—provided she was generous in her turn. To let him provide for her would have been the prudent course, and even a measure of revenge upon the Aldons for the wrong they had done her, and yet she had cast it irrevocably aside. Not because she set too high a value upon her virtue, but because she could not bring herself to surrender it to a youth she so heartily despised. That would indeed be a betrayal of herself.

She sighed and laid aside the comb, and sat watching her tame rabbit as it nibbled a handful of green leaves at her feet. Self-mockery swept over her as she realised the futility of her thoughts. She had not yet broken herself of the habit of thinking like Sir Edwin Aldon's foster-daughter, to whom wealth and security made the preserving or surrendering of virtue a matter of inclination rather than harsh necessity. Alone and unprotected, she would have to be extraordinarily fortunate to be given any choice in the matter at all.

A distant clamour broke in upon her thoughts, the sound of many voices raised in anger or dispute. It seemed to come from the direction of the village, but as she listened, wondering a little uneasily what it portended, she realised that it was drawing rapidly nearer. Her uneasiness increased and she rose to her feet, then, seeing that the rabbit had stopped feeding and now sat with sensitive ears pricked forward and nose a-quiver, stooped to take the little creature up in her arms.

The noise was so near now that she could hear something of what the angry voices were shouting; the dread word "witch" reached her ears, and for a few moments sheer panic paralysed mind and body, so that she stood motionless by the stool from which she had risen, unable to move or even to think. Then, as the shouting drew closer, she sprang into instinctive flight, but even as she reached the open door the mob of villagers surged round the bend of the lane, and its leader loosed a yell of triumph at sight of her.

They came crowding into the garden; men, women and even children, all fear of her forgotten, thrusting and elbowing their way forward until they were clustered close about the doorway, and every chance of escape was gone. Bronwen, finding herself cornered, beat down the rising waves of panic and tried to face them calmly.

"Why are you here?" she asked them. "What do you want of me?"

At the sound of her voice most of them fell silent, each looking one to the other, for it was still the voice of "Miss Bronwen from the Hall", and the habit of respect died hard. Then the man who seemed to be their leader, and whom Bronwen recognised as the chief of the servants whom Sir John Aldon had brought with him to Twyning Hall, thrust his way forward. He was a big, arrogant fellow named Thomas Barnes, greatly trusted by Sir John and with a high opinion of his own importance.

"We're here to rid ourselves o' witchcraft," he said

aggressively. "Of you, and your damned trafficking with the Devil."

"I am no witch," she replied angrily. "This is mere folly, born of ignorance and malice." She raised her voice a little, addressing them all. "Good people, I have dwelt among you all my life, and what harm have I ever done to any of you?"

"Harm enough to my master's family," Barnes retorted. "You killed poor young Mr. Francis, just as you said you would."

The whole world seemed to spin madly around her. She put out one hand to grasp the door-post, and said faintly:

"Francis . . . dead?"

"Aye, as well you know! Thrown from his horse as he rode with his brother this morning, and his neck broke, and his poor mother the first to see him when they carried his body home. Nigh out of her mind with grief, my lady is!"

" 'Er said as 'er would do it! Me and Meg heard her!" It was a child's voice now, shrill with excitement and importance. "Yesterday, out yonder in the lane! 'You'll never live to be a man,' 'er said!"

Bronwen's dazed glance sought out the speaker; saw a skinny, brown-faced lad pointing an accusing finger; remembered the boy and girl peering from the bushes at her angry, contemptuous parting from Francis the day before. Then the child's mother dragged him back and placed herself in front of him, one hand stretched out towards Bronwen, the fist clenched and first and last finger extended in the ancient gesture to ward off evil.

"And that's not the only threat she made," Thomas Barnes added. "She threatened Sir John himself when he turned her out of the Hall. Laid a curse on him and all his family! It's begun, neighbours! Mr. Francis is dead. Do we mean to let it go on?"

A roar of approval greeted his words, and from the back of the crowd someone cried: "The Bible says 'thou shalt not suffer a witch to live.' "

"I am no witch!" Bronwen repeated, but now there was a ragged edge of panic to her voice. "I did not threaten Francis. I taunted him, that is all. The children misunderstood what I said."

"And did Sir John and my lady misunderstand when you told them the name of Aldon would perish and be known no more?" Barnes demanded. "Her ladyship was that stricken she took to her bed, but she told her waiting-woman what ailed her, and the waiting-woman told the rest of us. There's no doubt of it, neighbours! She's a black witch, and not one of us'll be safe till we're rid of her."

There were cries of agreement and a threatening, forward surge of the crowd. Bronwen recoiled and looked frantically about for some way of escape, tossing back her long, loose hair. In doing so she revealed for the first time the rabbit which all this while she had been clasping to her bosom with her left hand, and at sight of the little creature, one of the women let out a shriek.

"Look! Look! She holds her imp in her arms! And she says she be no witch!"

The forward movement checked abruptly, and a mutter ran through the crowd, a sound eloquent now of fear as well as hatred. It was a common belief that witches kept imps or familiar demons in the shape of small animals, which they sent out to cause death and disaster among their neighbours. Everyone had heard of such imps, but hearing of them was one thing; being confronted by one was another, and for a moment their fury was tempered by awe. Then came Thomas Barnes's voice again to spur them on.

"Mr. Mark said it was a rabbit caused his brother's horse to bolt. The witch's imp, neighbours, sent to kill the poor young gentleman. Seize the Devil's hag!"

Suiting action to the words, he sprang forward and caught Bronwen by the arm as she tried to retreat into the cottage. The rabbit, leaping from her slackened grip, darted in blind terror between the legs of the crowd and disappeared into the tangled weeds of the garden, and with its going the courage of the mob returned. Barnes dragged Bronwen out from the doorway, and in an instant she was surrounded by the yelling, struggling villagers. Hands clawed at her, tugging at her hair, ripping her garments; blows rained upon her so that she was beaten to her knees, seeking feebly to protect her head and face with upraised arms. It seemed that she would be battered to death on the spot, but Barnes, aided by the blacksmith, fended off the attack and hauled her to her feet, holding her captive by each grasping one of her wrists. With his free hand Barnes seized her hair, twisting his fingers into it at the nape of the neck and wrenching her head cruelly back.

"Murdering hell-hag!" he said viciously. "Do you still deny traffic with the Devil?"

"Her can't deny it," one of the women said in an awed tone. "He've set his mark on her. Look!"

They followed the direction of the pointing finger. In the assault on her, Bronwen's clothing had been torn from the upper part of her body, and all could see, just below her left breast, a curiously shaped birthmark dark against the white skin. As they stared, the woman who had first perceived it said in a hushed voice:

"A horned head! That be the Devil's mark, for sure."

"For sure," Barnes repeated jeeringly, "but lest there be any that still doubt it, we'll put her to one more test. Come, friends! We'll swim the witch in the pool below the mill."

This proposal was greeted with enthusiasm, and the whole crowd at once began to stream out of the garden towards the village, Bronwen being dragged along in their midst by her two captors. One or two of the young men lingered long enough to venture into the cottage, kindle brands at the fire and set these to furniture, and thatch before hastening after their companions. Behind them, smoke began to billow from door and windows, and a faint, crackling sound told of the flames taking hold.

Bronwen, stumbling along between Barnes and the smith, heard the men shouting triumphantly to the rest of the crowd that they had burned the witch's lair, but this no longer seemed of any importance. Her mind was filled, overwhelmed, possessed by terror of what lay before her. "Swim the witch." She had heard that phrase before, and knew only too well the horror those simple words implied; it was an ancient and widely accepted test for anyone suspected of witchcraft. When they came to the pool, she would be stripped and bound, left hand to right foot and right to left, before being flung into the deep water. In the unlikely event of her floating, her guilt would be established and she would be hauled out and dragged off to be tried and executed. Drowning was a far more probable and possibly more merciful fate.

At first there was no room in her thoughts for hope, for the idea of escape, but as they passed through the village she realised that she and her captors had fallen a little behind the others, or rather, that the rest of the crowd, eager for the spectacle which was to be afforded them, had hurried on ahead. In the midst of the village, just beyond the green, the street forked, the left-hand track leading to the mill and the right passing between the forge and the inn towards the forest a quarter of a mile away. Barnes and the smith were paying little heed to her; she had ceased to struggle, and their grip on her arms was only firm enough to pull her along between them. As they reached the spot where the two ways met she suddenly wrenched herself free, taking them both completely by surprise, and plunged desperately along the right-hand track. Luck was with her. Both men dived in pursuit, collided violently and went down in a struggling, cursing heap.

Bronwen fled past the inn, past the last, scattered cottages and along the dusty, winding, gently sloping track. Behind her sounded the angry shouts, first the voices of Barnes and the smith, and then, joining them, the furious yells of the rest of the villagers. Driven by terror, she ran as she had never run in her life, towards the dark wall of the forest which offered at least an illusion of sanctuary. Her breath came in great, tearing gasps, and a pain as sharp as a sword-blade pierced her side, but she forced her trembling limbs onward. Stumbling, reeling, almost blind with exhaustion, but driven to even greater efforts by the hideous, scarcely human clamour of the pursuit, she fled for her life beneath the storm-dark sky, while lightning stabbed the clouds and thunder rolled and rumbled overhead.

Part Three

The storm, as brief as it was violent, had passed by the time Bronwen finished her story. The sky was growing lighter, the thunder had rumbled away into the distance, and the stillness of the forest was broken only by the drip of raindrops from the leaves and the occasional call of a bird. In the sheltered corner of the ruins, too, there was silence for a space after Bronwen's quiet voice ceased. She had told her story calmly, unemotionally, as though it concerned someone other than herself, because that was the only way in which, as yet, she could bring herself to think of it. As something which had no part in the present moment, no connection with the rain-washed, sweet-scented peace of the forest, the ancient calm of the crumbling walls, or the compassion in the dark eyes of Benedict Forde—a compassion oddly at variance with the rest of his swarthy, cynical face. Deliberately she had thrown up a barrier against memory, for to recall too vividly the ordeal through which she had lately passed would be to remember also that she was homeless, hunted and in peril of her life; and that way lay panic and despair.

"So there you have it," she said at length, in the same dead, toneless voice. "In the eyes of those people I am a proven witch, a harbourer of demons, a bringer of death. Perhaps in your eyes also, now that you have heard my story."

"Conjure me a demon, or fly above yon treetops, and I will admit your witch-hood," he said ironically. "My poor child, if you possessed such powers as they accuse you of, I fancy Sir John Aldon would have lain dead these many weeks. However, there is no denying the danger in which you stand. Women have been tried and convicted upon less so-called evidence than now stands against you, and those who sit in judgment are no less gullible than the rustics from whom you fled. The Bible tells us we must not suffer a witch to live, therefore to deny the existence of witches is to cast doubt upon Holy Writ. A dangerous thing to do."

There was a satirical inflection to his voice; Bronwen's gaze searched his face. "Yet you deny it?"

"I deny nothing. I have seen too many strange things in the course of my life, things which cannot be explained. What I do find hard to credit is that women possessed of such hellish powers would meekly suffer themselves to be imprisoned, tortured and hanged. Or that the Devil would so often choose as his minions the old and the poor, with opportunity to wreak no greater evil than the wasting of a neighbour's cattle or the blighting of his crops."

"So Sir Edwin argued," Bronwen agreed with a sigh, "years ago when old Abby was accused." She shivered. "I fear such arguments will avail me no more than they availed her."

"Argument is of little use against ignorance and superstition. You have been marvellously misfortunate, Bronwen. Your foster-father's love of learning, your own distress when his books were burned, young Francis's fatal accident after the children misheard what you said to him. It is easy to see how your neighbours' fears battened upon these things until they were ready to believe that you cherish an imp of hell, and bear the Devil's mark upon your body."

"I do bear such a mark," she said in a low voice. "My misfortune is that they should have discovered it."

He looked sceptical. "The mark of a horned head?"

"It could be taken as such, if one wished to believe it. My mother bore it, too, just as I do."

"Then you knew your mother?"

She shook her head. "No, nor anything about her save that her name was Bronwen. Twenty years ago Sir Edwin, returning from his travels, was in a village on the coast at the time of a great storm. A ship foundered within sight of the shore, and none escaped save one young man who came staggering from the sea with the body of a woman in his arms. Sir Edwin, who had gone to the beach with the men of the village, tried to succour him, but he was beyond mortal aid. He spoke only once before he died. He said, "care for Bronwen.""

"At first they thought the woman was dead, too, but

then they found that she still breathed. Sir Edwin had them carry her to the inn where he was lodged, and since he was skilled in medicine he succeeded in keeping her alive. For days she lay between life and death, and when at last she regained her senses she could remember nothing. Not who she was, or whence she came, or whither she had been bound. Sir Edwin assumed that the man who saved her from the shipwreck was her lover, since, though she was big with child, she wore no marriage-ring. When she was strong enough to travel he brought her to Twyning Hall, and there, two months later, I was born and my mother died."

"And did she never recover her memory?"

Bronwen shook her head. "Whatever the truth of her identity, its secret went with her to the grave. Sir Edwin gave me her name and had me reared as though I were his own child. He had never married and had little liking for the company of his fellow men, but, in his fashion, he loved me. He left me generously provided for, but, as I told you, his kinsmen challenged the Will and the courts supported their claim."

"And now, not content with having lawfully robbed you of your inheritance," Benedict concluded dryly, "it appears that they seek lawfully to murder you, for it seems to me that there is overmuch of this servant of theirs in this day's events."

"You mean Thomas Barnes? Yes, he was the ringleader, though whether or not at his master's bidding I do not know. It may be that the man honestly believes me guilty of witchcraft."

"It may be that Sir John Aldon and his family honestly believe it," Benedict replied cynically, "but that does not alter the fact that your death would rid them of an embarrassment. By now they will have learned of your escape and the hunt will be up in earnest. Are we likely to be looked for here?"

"In this place?" She shook her head. "These ruins have too evil a reputation."

He looked amused. "All the more reason, surely, for a fugitive witch to take refuge in them? Will not the village think of that?"

"They might think of it, but not one of them would venture here by night, and probably not even by day. This part of the forest was cultivated land once, belonging to a convent, but the holy sisters, so the story goes, turned from piety into lewd and sinful ways, and God destroyed both them and the church they had profaned. Now their unquiet spirits haunt the place."

He detected an undertone of mockery in her voice. "You do not believe it?"

She shrugged. "There *was* a convent here, and it was destroyed. That much is certain, so that much I believe."

He rose to his feet and stood looking about him. She watched him curiously, but could detect no trace of uneasiness in his face. At length he said:

"So you will not fear to bide here until morning?"

"No." She spoke calmly, still watching him. "Will you?"

He chuckled. "No, faith, not I! I would I could offer you more comfortable lodging, but it will not do to seek shelter at an inn if the Aldons have roused the countryside against you. It will soon be dark, so, while some light remains, I will take what measures I can for your comfort."

He took off his sword and shoulder-belt, propping the sheathed weapon against the wall, and went out through the archway and across the clearing to the forest. In the open the grass was soaked, but though the rain had been heavy it had not lasted long enough to penetrate the heavy, summer foliage, and deep beneath the trees the undergrowth was still dry. Benedict gathered an armful of bracken and carried it back and dropped it beside Bronwen before returning for a second load.

Although the storm had freshened the air, it was still very warm. He had already discarded his hat and cloak, and before long he was glad to remove his doublet also and roll up the ruffled sleeves of his shirt, but he went on collecting bracken until there was a great pile of it heaped in the sheltered corner of the ruined chapel. He picked up his cloak and spread it on top of the pile.

"That will have to serve you for a bed," he told Bronwen. "I regret it is no better."

Her strange, slanted eyes lifted to meet his. "I might have lain in a prison cell this night," she said in a low voice. "That is, if I had survived the ordeal in the pool. I owe my life to you, Benedict Forde, and I am well aware that there are not many men who would have come to the aid of one branded a witch."

He made no reply to this beyond suggesting that she should seat herself on the couch of bracken, and went to take from one of his saddle-bags a bottle of wine, and some bread, meat and cheese wrapped in a white cloth. Bronwen looked at the provisions in surprise.

"Food also?" she said. "Did you intend to spend the night out of doors?"

"I intended to bespeak a bed at an inn, but it has become a habit with me to furnish myself with food and drink before setting out on a day's march." He cast her a humorous glance. "One never knows what may chance on a journey."

"A day's march," she repeated, and added curiously: "Are you a soldier?"

There was a brief pause before he replied. He spread the provisions on the cloth on top of a flat piece of fallen stone, took out a knife, and quizzically regarded the bright blade as though debating with himself what answer to make. At length he said:

"I have been many things, Bronwen. A soldier was one of them."

She waited for him to say more, but he seemed to consider this answer enough, and went on with his preparations for the simple meal. She bit her lip at the rebuff, and was conscious of a feeling of desolation. There was no reason in the world why he should satisfy her curiosity, but in her present terrible and frightening loneliness she felt an urgent need to establish some relationship, however tenuous, with the one person who had shown her kindness. The grim events of the evening were taking their toll; she felt battered and bone-weary and utterly wretched.

Although she had not eaten since noon, and then only frugally, she found herself unable to force down more than a few morsels of the food Benedict offered, and to swallow a mouthful or two of the wine. He looked searchingly at her when she refused to take more, but made no comment. There was silence between them for a while, and then he remarked:

"There is one thing, Bronwen, which puzzles me. Those children misunderstood your words to Francis Aldon and twisted them into a threat against his life, but what of the thing you said to Sir John and his lady, about the name of Aldon being known no more?"

She did not reply at once, but toyed with a frond of the bracken on which she sat, drawing it gently through her fingers and watching it spring back into shape.

"That *will* come to pass," she said reluctantly at last. "I have seen it. New tombs in the church, and cold grey ashes blowing down the wind."

"You have *seen* it?" He regarded her dubiously, as though uncertain whether or not to take her words seriously. "Would you have me believe that you are indeed a witch?"

"If I am, it is not through choice," she replied. "I am no scryer, peering into mirrors or pools of ink to plunder the future of its secrets. When the knowledge comes, it comes in spite of me, unsought and unwanted, but the fact remains that as I spoke with Sir John I saw what I have just described to you. As I have seen other things at intervals during my life. Things which have always come to pass."

The lack of emphasis, and the complete sincerity with which she spoke, convinced him that what she said was true. It was a measure of the man that he could accept this without scepticism and without fear.

"I have heard of such a gift," he said slowly, "but never encountered it until now." He frowned. "Does anyone else know of it?"

She shook her head. "The first time it happened I was only a child. It terrified me, and I fled to Sir Edwin for comfort. He warned me then never to speak of it to anyone, since men fear what they cannot understand, and seek to destroy that which they fear." She raised her head to look at him, and there was wonder in her next words, as though she were astonished at herself. "This is the first time I have ever disregarded that advice."

"Your secret is safe with me," Benedict replied in a low voice, "although I do not pretend to understand it."

They continued to look at each other through the gathering shadows, in a silence suddenly charged with more than a perilous secret shared. The light was fading fast, but he could still see her sitting on the billowing pile of bracken, her tattered green skirts spread about her, her white shoulders and bosom barely veiled by the mantle of her hair. Desire surged up within him, a fierce longing to possess this mysterious, elusive creature whose pale slenderness and haunting, strange-eyed face held a lure no plump beauty could have matched; who was his for the taking, isolated as they were in these ill-omened ruins buried deep in the forest. Yet, since for all his harsh cynicism he was not wholly unscrupulous, the very fact that she was defenceless set a curb on his passion, warning him of the remorse he would feel later if he gave rein to it. The victory was not easily won, and the force of conflicting emotions brought him to his feet, to stand staring down at her.

Bronwen continued to watch him, her head tilted back to look up at him as he towered above her. Interpreting correctly the expression in his face, she was frightened, yet aware, beneath the fear, of quickened pulses and a little stirring of excitement. She, too, was conscious of the loneliness of the place and the hour, and of the mounting tide of feeling between them.

In the dimness behind them the horse moved suddenly, so that its iron-shod hooves rang on the stone floor, and the sound shattered the growing tension. Bronwen started and uttered a little cry, and Benedict, turning sharp on his heel, strode away under the broken archway and out of sight.

.   .   .   .   .   .

Bronwen was dreaming, and in her dream she lived again the terror of the witch-hunt. Heard the hoarse, shrill, hate-filled voices, felt the brutal hands, was dragged again towards the unthinkable ordeal of the water; but in her dream she did not escape. In her dream she was hauled to the very verge of the pool; felt her clothing being torn from her, and the ropes harsh about wrists and ankles, wrenching her limbs cruelly into unnatural distortion; stared down into the cold, green depths of the pool where weeds writhed like sinuous, waiting arms. Struggled with futile, mounting panic—and started awake to find herself sitting bolt upright on the bed of bracken, with tears streaming down her cheeks.

So vivid was the dream, so real the horror, that several seconds passed before she realised that it was, in fact, no more than a dream. She could not remember where she was, and stared wildly about her. At the moonlight streaming through the broken tracery of a window above her to spill a silvery pool of brightness on the flagstones just beyond where she sat; at the shadows which seemed blacker yet by contrast; at the white mist that drifted, waist-high, in that part of the chapel open to the sky, and in the clearing glimpsed through the ruined archway.

After a few panic-stricken moments, memory returned. She was in the convent ruins, whither she had come with Benedict Forde after he rescued her from the witch-hunt, but where was her rescuer now? Utter stillness and silence enfolded her. The horse no longer shifted and snorted in the shadows, as it had done when she fell into exhausted sleep. There was no sense of any other living creature anywhere about her.

With a sob of despair she started up and stumbled towards the archway, for suddenly the ruins seemed hostile, no longer a sanctuary but a trap, and hideous phantoms mocked at her out of the darkness. At her first step something coiled itself about her feet and brought her to her knees, and she knew a moment's blind terror before she realised that this was the belt of Benedict's sword, which he had left propped against the wall.

With a rush of relief she realised that he could not completely have abandoned her, or else the weapon would no longer be there. Still on her knees in the patch of moonlight, she lifted the sheathed rapier and was about to restore it to its place when the smooth coldness of the hilt against her hand turned her thoughts in a new direction. Appalled by the idea which had flashed into her mind, she tried to banish it and could not. It took root, flourished, burgeoned into sinister life, tempting her with the promise of an end to all care. Why not? it whispered. What does life hold for you now?

Reluctantly, still striving to resist, she slowly drew the sword from its scabbard; three feet of tempered steel, deadly-pointed, its diamond-shaped blade razor sharp for two-thirds of its length. Held it before her, watching the dull, blue-white glimmer of the moonlight along it. Turned it about, placing the hilt against a crack between the flagstones on which she knelt. Shook back her hair, and guided the point towards her breast, where the small patch of the birthmark darkened the whiteness of her skin.

There was a swift, sudden movement behind her. An arm was flung round her, gripping her like a band of iron, pinning her own arms to her sides; she was jerked to her feet, the sword spinning from her hand. Benedict's deep voice, vibrant with shock and anger, said explosively:

"In God's name, girl! Are you mad?"

She struggled to free herself. "Let me go! Oh, why did you stop me? I am afraid! I cannot face it again, the mob, the water. I cannot!"

"Nor shall you!" He shifted his hold on her, swinging her to face him; his hands gripped her bare shoulders. "Did I not save you from the clutches of the mob? I will not abandon you to them again, and still less will I let you destroy yourself."

"What is it to you?" Although helpless in his grasp, she still sought furiously to break free. "Better death now, swift and merciful, than that which awaits me if I am taken. Better even than to live as I must live henceforth."

"Craven words," he said sternly, "and false, too. Life is not lightly to be cast aside, no matter to what depths of despair one has sunk. Believe me, I speak of what I know."

"Do you?" she demanded wildly. "Have *you* ever been destitute and hunted, in danger of your life?"

"Even so. And, as you see, I still live."

Still straining against his hold, both hands pressed against his chest to thrust him away, she stared resentfully up at him. In the bright moonlight his gaunt face looked more forbidding than ever, and the voice which had charmed and comforted was implacable now, condemning her weakness and demanding a courage she could not seem to find. Abruptly, all the defiance went out of her; she uttered a small, incoherent sound and collapsed against him. She was trembling violently.

"I am so afraid! I could face loneliness and poverty, but not to be named witch. To be hunted like an animal! Those people today would have killed me. They screamed for my death!"

He took her in his arms, holding her gently now, one hand stroking her hair. "I swear to you," he said quietly, "that you will never be taken as a witch. Aldon's influence is not so wide that we cannot journey beyond it, and until we have done so, trust me to keep you safe from him."

Resting against him, feeling the strong, steady beat of his heart beneath her cheek, she was soothed by a sense of comfort and protection, and as the vividness of her dream began to fade, so, too, did her dread of the reality from which the dream had sprung. Benedict Forde was right. The gift of life was too precious to be cast aside.

"Twice you have saved me," she murmured, "once from the villagers, and once from myself. Why should you protect me? Why burden yourself with the troubles of a stranger?"

He made no reply, but the rhythm of his heartbeats had quickened, the clasp of his arms about her become less gentle, and as she raised her head in instinctive protest his mouth came down on hers, stifling the words she had been about to utter, stopping her breath so that moonlight and shadow alike spun away into whirling darkness. After that first, brief movement she did not struggle, but forced herself to remain passive in his arms and utterly unresponsive to the urgent demands of lips and hands, until her very stillness gave him pause. He relaxed his hold a little and looked down at her as she lay back across his arm, her face drained of all colour in the moonlight, the black hair streaming back from her brow. She stared back at him from wide, slanted eyes, and he saw the gleam of tears on her cheeks.

"I have my answer!" Her voice was breathless and shaken, but infinitely contemptuous. "Like Francis, like all men, you demand but one thing as the price of your

65

protection." She moved her head in a weary, defenceless gesture. "Take your payment, then. I cannot prevent you."

For a few seconds longer he continued to regard her, and then he drew her erect and let her go. His face was grim with anger.

"You are a clever woman," he said bitterly. "Resistance I would have been tempted to overcome, but the making of martyrs has never appealed to me. Abate your fears! I shall not take you by force." He paused for a moment, and when he spoke again, his voice had changed; grown softer, more compelling. "You will come to me willingly, Bronwen, if you come at all."

"But if I do not," she whispered, "I may look elsewhere for aid. That is what you are saying, is it not?"

"No." Abruptly he stepped aside into the shadows where he had placed the saddle by the wall, groped for a moment, and then turned with a pistol in his hand. Examined the weapon briefly, then stepped to where Bronwen stood, watching him, her arms crossed upon her breast. Took her hand and closed the cold fingers firmly about the pistol butt.

"Handle it carefully," he warned her. "It is loaded, primed and cocked. You have but to aim it, and fire." He stepped back a few paces and stood facing her, hands resting lightly on his hips. "If I have lied to you, if I attempt you again, you have a sure means of preserving your virtue."

"Have I?" The mockery in her voice was like a faint echo of his. "I think you gamble upon my dread of the witch-hunt being the greater. If I killed you, who would protect me from that?"

He shrugged. "There is gold in my purse and a good horse grazing yonder. You could make your escape unaided."

There was a pause. The patch of moonlight in which they stood had shifted a fraction, and now frosted the edges of the heap of bracken and the folds of the cloak spread on it; a vagrant breeze rustled through the forest, stirred the mist into eerie ghost-shapes, and was gone; an owl hooted mournfully. Bronwen looked from the pistol in her hand to the man who so calmly confronted her, his white shirt, sharply defined against the darkness behind him, offering a target which at this range even an inexperienced aim could not miss.

"Come now!" the deep voice mocked her. "A little resolution and the thing is done."

Slowly she lifted the hand that held the pistol, and faced him across the levelled weapon. Faced, too, the choice which had been thrust upon her. Not of killing him, for that she could never do, but of denying or yielding to the tide of emotion which had been imperceptibly rising about them and now was running full and strong.

Yet there was no choice. This moment had been inevitable since their meeting at the forest's edge, with the witch-hunt howling and clamouring at her heels; since, here in the ruined chapel, she had told him her story; most of all, since she had felt his kisses on her lips and the force of his passion waking an answering desire in her.

So, for a long moment, they looked at each other in

silence, and then she lowered her hand, laid the pistol carefully aside, and went forward, across the patch of moonlight, into his arms.

•   •   •   •   •

Benedict stood in the archway and looked across the clearing at the first sunlight gilding the topmost branches of the trees. At ground level the mist still lay thick and white and the silence which lay over the forest was composed of all the small, woodland sounds of the awakening day. In the chapel behind him Bronwen was sleeping, wrapped in the cloak he had folded about her, her hair tumbled across the withering bracken which had been their pillow, but already the man's mind was occupied with the practical problems of carrying her out of danger.

These, he admitted to himself, were considerable. He had long been absent from England, but he knew that here, as in other lands, a witch-hunt would not be halted by a single reverse, especially when a powerful family like the Aldons was so intimately involved. If Sir John believed, as well he might, that his son's death had been brought about by Bronwen, he would have informed constables and magistrates for miles around and all would be on the alert to capture her, for murder by witchcraft was one of the most abhorred of all crimes.

Nor would Benedict's own presence, of itself, be sufficient to divert suspicion from her, for the villagers had seen him when he caught her up on to his horse, and some of them, at least, must be able to describe him. Knowing nothing of the supernatural origin ascribed to him by those same villagers, he assumed that Sir John would have made it known that the supposed witch had last been seen in company with a man dressed in black and scarlet, and riding a black horse.

It would be necessary, therefore, to move with extreme caution in providing for their immediate needs, since this must be done with as little delay as possible. He would have to obtain food, for though he had been careful to reserve some of the provisions, these were not sufficient to do more than remove the sharp edge of hunger; and fresh clothes for Bronwen, a disguise of some sort to replace the rags of her silken finery. Once that was done, they must make all haste away from the dangerous neighbourhood of Twyning Hall and the vengeance of the bereaved Sir John.

He went softly out of the chapel, satisfied himself that all was well with the horse, and then passed on to the stream, where he knelt to sluice the cool water over face and arms, ruefully fingering the black stubble of beard on his chin and reflecting that to appear thus villainously unshaven would do nothing to make his task easier. However, there was no help for that; he would have to trust to dress and manner to carry matters off with a high hand.

Returning presently to the chapel, he gently roused Bronwen. She blinked at him in sleepy bewilderment, and then alarm came leaping into her eyes. He spoke quickly to reassure her.

"There is naught to fear, sweeting, but it is past sunrise and we must soon be away."

She relaxed again and reached out a hand to him, but asked with a trace of wistfulness: "Away whither?"

"Why, anywhere, so that it be far from Sir John Aldon," he replied humorously, enfolding the hand in his own, "but first you will have to lead the way to more open country, for I confess myself lost in this maze of woodland. Can you do it? You guided us here unerringly last night."

"Yes, for the forest was my playground as a child, and the gypsies taught me many of its secret ways."

"The gypsies?" he repeated quizzically. "Now what the devil had Sir Edwin Aldon's foster-daughter to do with such vagabonds?"

"She had a deal to do with them," Bronwen retorted, "for Sir Edwin himself in no way despised them, and allowed them to camp upon his land whenever they wished. He spent much time with the old and wise among them, for he said they were a very ancient people with many curious traditions and secret lore, and he wished to learn of them. He was a man whose thirst for knowledge was never quenched."

She stopped abruptly and turned her head away, biting her lip. Benedict guessed the trend of her thoughts.

"Bronwen, no repining can ever recall the past or change the present," he said gently.

She sighed. "Yes, you are right. To repine is useless, a waste of time which could be better employed." She freed her hand from his and sat up, making a little grimace of pain. "My good neighbours yesterday used me more roughly than I realised. I am bruised from head to foot."

He helped her up and stood, supporting her with an

arm about her waist, regarding her with some anxiety. "Will you be able to ride?"

"Well enough, once this stiffness had passed. Believe me, I would endure far greater discomfort in order to escape pursuit of the kind you saved me from." She smiled, and lifted her hand briefly to touch his cheek. "Do not fear that I shall hinder our flight for so slight a cause."

He did not dispute the matter, though he thought it likely that for all her brave words she would not be able to face many hours of travelling that day. He would have felt easier in his mind had he known how far they would have to go before they might consider themselves safe from recognition and pursuit, and how close a watch was being kept for them.

He was still wrestling with this problem as they shared the remains of the food, and seemed so grimly preoccupied that Bronwen hesitated to break in upon his thoughts. At last she said diffidently:

"In which direction do you mean to travel? That must be decided before we set out, so that I know which path to follow through the forest."

He looked wryly at her. "I know, but the devil of it is that I have no means of telling which way it is best to go, save that we must give wide berth to the village of Twyning Green."

There was a pause, and then she spoke more hesitantly then before. "Whither were you bound when we met? You must wish to complete that journey, and I have no right to ask that you turn aside from it for my sake."

"No need to ask it, either," he said with a smile. "I

was on my way to Suffolk, where my kinfolk dwell, but whether that journey is completed in a day, or a month, or never, matters not at all."

"But are you not looked for there?"

He laughed. "It would be marvellous indeed if I were. It is twenty years since I last saw the place, and no one there knows whether I am alive or dead. Nor cares, either, I'll wager!"

"Twenty years?" she repeated disbelievingly. "You can have been no more than a child then."

"I was fifteen. My father, as fathers will, had laid down the course my life was to follow, but I had the impertinence to disagree, believing that I knew, better than he, whether or not I was suited to the profession he was determined I should take up. I still believe it." He paused, and Bronwen saw a gleam of sardonic humour in his eyes. "He intended me for the Church."

She stared blankly at him, for whatever Benedict Forde had been like at the age of fifteen, it was impossible to look at him at thirty-five and imagine him in Holy Orders. With his harsh, dark face and sombre yet flamboyant dress he looked, she thought (unknowingly echoing the opinion of her pursuers the previous evening), more like an emissary of the powers of darkness.

"Yes," Benedict said with a touch of amusement, "*you* perceive the absurdity of such a notion. My father would not, and demanded an obedience I was not prepared to give. As the youngest son of a youngest son I was willing to make my own way in the world, but not as a country parson. He remained adamant, so I took the only alternative, and ran away from home. I

72

was well-grown for my age and of a cast of countenance which made me seem older than my years, and I knew I could pass easily for seventeen or eighteen. I went secretly from the house, took my horse, and a sword I scarcely knew how to use, and with only a few shillings in my pocket, set out to seek my fortune."

"And now," Bronwen concluded as he paused, "having found it, are you returning home in triumph?"

"That would be an apt ending to the tale, would it not? Unhappily, matters have not fallen out so. I have known what it is to be very rich, and very poor. I have lived like a prince, and as a slave. I have roamed through most of the countries of the world. Now I am returning home very much as I left, with a horse, and a sword . . ."

"And with gold in your purse," she reminded him ironically. "Or so you told me last night."

He laughed. "True! That distorts the picture a little, does it not? But my present fortune amounts to no more than a few hundred pounds. I ride homeward in the hope of increasing it."

Bronwen blinked. "Faith, but you are sanguine! After twenty years' absence, do you look to be welcomed?"

"Stranger things befall. A month since I found myself in France, where, as you may know, are many Englishmen who find it prudent or desirable to be out of England while Cromwell and his army rule. Among these was one who knew my family well, and from him I learned that through war and pestilence and the mere passage of time, its number is now reduced to my uncle—my father's elder brother—his grand-daughter, and her widowed mother. My own father and brothers, my uncle's two sons, all are dead. Do you not think, therefore, that my uncle will be overjoyed to learn that one man of his blood still lives? Even if he is not, I am at least entitled to my father's share of the family property."

"Unless," she said shrewdly, "your father willed it elsewhere as punishment for your defiance. Had you not thought of that?"

The food and wine were finished. Benedict rose to his feet and stretched out his hand to help her up also, pulling her into his arms.

"I had," he replied laconically, "and from what I remember of my honoured sire it seems more than likely, but I do not lose hope on that account. My uncle is growing old, and has no one but a slip of a girl to succeed him. I was always on good terms with him, and it should not be difficult to persuade him to reinstate me. Then the future will be assured." He looked down into Bronwen's upraised face and strange, beautiful eyes, and his arms tightened about her. "But that is for later. What matters to me now is to keep you safe, so let us begone from here."

He kissed her quickly and let her go, turning away to pick up his sword. Bronwen made as though to speak, for there was one more question she wanted to ask, but he took up the saddle and went out before she could find the words. She stood for a few moments looking after him, and then sighed and began to gather together the traces of their meal. When these had been disposed of, she twisted her hair into a thick braid, fastened Benedict's cloak about her, and after a last, lin-

74

gering look around the chapel, went out under the archway to join him.

.　　　.　　　.　　　.　　　.

They had been some time upon their way before she found the courage to ask her question. Benedict had decided to strike out in exactly the opposite direction to the one by which they had come, so that they might put as great a distance as possible between themselves and Twyning Green. As before, there was no visible path, but Bronwen, mounted again before him, guided the horse without hesitation until a track was reached.

Benedict looked back then, the way they had come, but there was no sign of their passing. The sea of bracken stretched, apparently unbroken, between the towering columns of the tree-trunks, and the ruins where they had spent the night were long since lost to view, buried and forgotten in this ocean of greenery. Already the place seemed unsubstantial as a dream. It was as though the girl who rode before him was indeed an elf-queen who had led him for a space out of the world of men into a realm unbounded by time or mortal laws.

He frowned, finding that he had to make a deliberate effort to shake off that sudden sense of unreality, as shake it off he must if they were to evade the dangers which now beset them. Bronwen said:

"This track runs roughly from east to west. The Hall and the village lie to the south-east."

"Then we ride westward," he replied, and turned the horse in that direction. "We will avoid the villages for as long as we may, and trust that by the time we are obliged to approach one we shall have outstripped news of what happened yesterday at Twyning Green."

She assented, but absently, and some time passed before she spoke again. At last, as though the question could remain unasked no longer, she said abruptly:

"Benedict, what did you mean last night when you said that your soul was damned beyond all hope of salvation?"

"Did I say that?" His tone was quizzical. "I think not, sweetheart. I said that those whose Christian beliefs led them to brand you a witch would, by those same beliefs, account me damned."

She leaned sideways a little to look up at him with a puzzled frown. "Is there a difference?"

"All the difference in the world. *I* do not believe myself so doomed, even though for seven years I bowed down in worship before the Crescent, and not the Cross."

"The Crescent?" she repeated blankly. "The Crescent of Islam?"

"Even so." He smiled down into her startled face. "Sir Edwin taught you much, did he not? Did he tell you also of the Barbary corsairs?"

"Of course. Has not all England heard of them? Benedict, do you mean that you were one of them?"

He nodded. "I commanded a galley in the service of the Bey of Algiers, and might have ended my days a Muslim had I not fallen foul of one who wielded great power and influence. For my life's sake I was obliged to leave the Barbary coast, and after various adven-

76

tures and misadventures drifted back to Europe and donned once more the mask of Christianity."

"The mask of Christianity?" she questioned gravely. "Is it no more to you than that?"

"Nothing more," he said with finality, "but do not suppose therefore that I am a devout Muslim. The one faith means as little to me as the other." He raised an ironical eyebrow. "What, do you not shrink in horror from such ungodliness?"

"Had I been reared in strict, God-fearing ways I might do so," she replied, "but Sir Edwin was not, by ordinary standards, a godly man. Unlike his kinsmen, who pride themselves on living by the word of Holy Writ yet see no wrong in robbing me, he doubted and questioned. He was prudent enough to hide his doubts from everyone save me, but he would not have me grow up in a blind faith he could not share. As for the Muslims, he visited Islam during the travels of his youth, and it was his belief that there is truth and holiness in that faith as in ours."

"There is evil and tyranny and greed in both also," Benedict said grimly. "I sailed in English ships, Bronwen, long before I came to Africa. I was flogged, half starved and compelled to face all kinds of peril to fill the pockets of some fat merchant in England who no doubt accounted himself a godly man. Then, in the West Indies, which His Holiness the Pope has seen fit to decree the sole possession of Catholic Spain, my ship fell into the hands of the Dons, and I and those others who survived the fight were made prisoner. Our captors were homeward bound for Spain, and there, as heretics, we were handed over to the Inquisition, which tortures men's bodies to save their souls."

She caught her breath and her hand tightened on his arm. "They tortured you?"

He shook his head. "I gave them no cause. There *are* matters for which I would suffer torment and death, but the Protestant faith was never one of them, and so with very little persuasion I became a convert to the Catholic Church. After due instruction I did public penance for my heresy and, thus purged of my sin, was suffered to depart—only to find myself seized by the secular arm and charged with piracy. I was convicted and condemned to the galleys."

He paused there, and she saw his face grow sombre with memories she could not even imagine; with recollections of a time which, she guessed, had done more than anything else to make him what he now was. At that moment he seemed utterly remote from her, a wanderer in a world of such vast misery and suffering that her own trials and terrors were suddenly insignificant.

"In those hell-ships," he resumed at last, "I learned something more of Christian's gentle way with Christian. For nearly a year I endured it. Labour such as I had never even imagined, filth, starvation, the constant bite of the lash. In the galleys the only fortunates are those too weak to survive. I was not. Already strong and hardy—for sea-faring breeds no weaklings—I found my strength increasing to meet the demands made on it. Then we were attacked by two corsair galleys. I broke free during the fight, and it pleases me to recall that I repaid in some measure the suffering I had

78

been forced to endure. In doing so, I saved the life of the corsair leader, himself a renegade Englishman, and in return he offered me freedom and a place in his crew if I would turn Muslim. I agreed. I would have struck a bargain with the Devil himself to escape from slavery, and besides, I had had a surfeit of Christianity, and the barbarities practised in Christ's gentle name." He laughed shortly, without humour. "I was soon to discover that, in this respect, there is little to choose between Christian and Muslim."

"Did you suffer greatly in Barbary also?" Bronwen asked compassionately, but Benedict shook his head.

"No, I was well treated, and I prospered, rising soon to a position of command and amassing considerable wealth. There are men of many European nations among the corsairs, but the Barbary princes value the English above all others. It seems we have the greatest talent for piracy." He paused, and when he spoke again the irony which had invested his previous words had faded from his voice. "But I saw barbarities practised in the name of Allah as great, and greater, than those I had suffered at Christian hands—aye, and came to practise some of them myself. Man is vile, Bronwen, by whatever name he calls his God, and God himself, if he exists at all, a blind, uncaring power indifferent to man's evil and man's suffering."

Bronwen was silent, not knowing how to reply. She felt neither disgust nor fear at what, to most people, would have seemed the most dreadful blasphemy, but only an overwhelming compassion for this man whom life had robbed of faith of any kind. Her own faith was strong, for all Sir Edwin's learning, all his wide tolerance of other men's beliefs, had never shaken his own faith in God. All his doubts and questions had been of the manner in which men worshipped Him, and of the bigotry and intolerance which led to conflict between them.

Sir Edwin's God was universal, the Supreme Being, the Many in One, the jewel of which each faith and creed could see but a single facet; and this belief he had bequeathed to Bronwen. It was a dangerous legacy. Sir Edwin, wise in the ways of his fellow men, had impressed upon his foster-child the need to cherish her faith in secret, to speak of it to no one. She had never done so, and even now, when every instinct was urging her to share it, some lingering caution held her back. She wanted to bring comfort to Benedict, to solace the bitterness and disillusion she sensed behind the cynical words, but something told her that to speak of her own beliefs would not help him; that the wound was too deep and poisonous to be so easily healed—if, indeed, it were not beyond all healing. Yet she could not let him think that his denial of God would indeed cause her to shrink from him. She sought for words to tell him so, then, finding none, reached up to clasp her arms about his neck and draw his face down to hers.

So for a while they rode locked in a close embrace, while the black horse, pacing slowly, went as it would through sunshine and shadow under the arching trees. It was the animal which first became aware of others in the forest besides themselves; of other men and other horses. It pricked its ears and whinnied, and from no great distance, like an echo, came the shrill reply.

Jerked abruptly back to reality, Bronwen and Benedict responded each in characteristic fashion: she with apprehension, with sharp dread of another witch-hunt; he transformed in an instant from lover to fighting-man, alert, keen-eyed, ready to fight or to retreat as circumstances might demand. The moments passed, taut with mounting tension, bringing to their ears the sound of an approaching company. A considerable company, for they could hear creaking wheels, the jingle of harness, the voices of men and women, the shrill trebles of children. Benedict glanced quickly about him, but the forest at this point was open, offering no concealment for a horse and riders. Whatever danger approached, if danger it were, they must either face it or fly from it.

The approaching company came into sight, along a path which wound up from a hollow on their left, a straggling line of wagons, pack-ponies, people afoot. Proud, dark people, arrogant of gait and fierce of face, clad in a kaleidoscope of colours which wound among the trees like a faded rainbow. Bronwen gave a gasp of relief.

"Gypsies! And I know that painted wagon at the head of the line. Benedict, they will help us!"

"It's to be hoped they will, sweetheart, for they are too many for me to do battle with, and to fly from them would drive us back towards Twyning Green, which is the last thing we desire. See, they have sighted us! Do we ride to meet them?"

"It would be best, I think, for they have no respect for those who show fear of them. Yet go warily. They are a people who have been persecuted for centuries, and to them a velvet doublet, a sword and a plume are

81

present symbols of that persecution. When we come within earshot I will speak to them in their own tongue, and then all will be well."

Benedict looked sceptical, but he shrugged slightly and urged the horse on again at the same easy pace as before. Although he would defend himself and Bronwen to the uttermost limit of his strength if it became necessary, he still retained much of the fatalism of Islam. What was to be, would be.

The cavalcade had not faltered in its slow advance, but, almost imperceptibly, a change was taking place in its formation. Women and children were falling back, men moving forward, until they marched shoulder to shoulder on either side of the painted cart, with more of their fellows in a close-packed group behind it. Not one threatening gesture was made, and yet there was something menacing in that silent ebb and flow of movement.

When only a score of yards lay between the head of the cavalcade and the doubly burdened horse, Bronwen called out a greeting in a strange tongue, adding something of which Benedict could understand only her own name and that of Sir Edwin Aldon. This seemed to produce some excitement among the gypsies, and when the horse drew level with the cart, the latter halted while the man sitting in it returned the greeting with dignity and a sort of aloof friendliness.

While the unintelligible conversation flowed past him, Benedict studied the gypsy leader. He was a giant of a man in early middle-age, black-bearded, with glittering dark eyes and a handsome, swarthy hawk-face. As Bronwen spoke quickly and urgently, he interpolated an occasional question, and more than once the piercing glance shifted to Benedict himself. Benedict met it coolly, without arrogance and without fear, and when the tale was done, the gypsy addressed him in English.

"You are welcome among us. Sir Edwin Aldon was ever a true friend to the Romany, and so is his foster-child. Last night we made camp upon Aldon land, as we have done ever since I was a boy, but we were driven forth with blows and curses. Now we go to another place we know, a secret place hidden deep in the forest. We have little enough, *rai*, but you saved the life of our friend and what we have is yours."

"My thanks to you," Benedict replied courteously. "We will gladly go with you, for this lady's danger is still very great. When we come to your camping-place, I will leave her in your care and go forth to discover where she may have the best chance of safety."

The gypsy shook his head. "The danger is everywhere, *rai*, for you as well as for her. In the village they speak with awe of a witch carried off by the Devil, but from the Hall the word goes out to seek a man clad in black and scarlet, riding a black horse."

"Damnation!" Benedict said softly. "I feared it might be so." He looked down at Bronwen. "It seems I am likely to bring you even greater danger. It were better that you take refuge with these good people for a time, while I try to lead the hunt on a fool's errand."

She uttered an exclamation of protest and distress, and her hand came up in a little, pleading gesture to clutch the front of his doublet. The gypsy leader, looking from one to the other, said calmly:

"It were better, *rai*, for you both to remain with us. Set aside those brave garments, the velvet and the plume, don rags such as we wear, and lose yourself among our company. My women will find clothes for Miss Bronwen. Those who seek you, seek one man and one woman. They will pay no more heed to a company of gypsies than is needful to drive them on their way."

Benedict nodded. "A good thought, friend! What of my horse?"

"It, too, may pass unnoticed among our own," the gypsy replied, and the hint of a grim smile touched the bearded lips, "for even a horse can be disguised. That is one of our secrets, *rai*, but we shall gladly use it to help our friend."

"Please, Benedict," Bronwen whispered, "do not leave me. I have such need of you."

He smiled reassuringly down at her. "Peace, sweeting," he said gently. "I shall not leave you unless my presence seems likely to add to your danger, and even then, be sure I should return. Meanwhile, our friend here gives good counsel. For the present, we shall become gypsies."

Part Four

For almost a month Bronwen and Benedict stayed with the Romany tribe. Benedict's original intention had been to remain in hiding for only a few days, but he learned that the search for him and his companion was being conducted with unusual vigour. Once disguised, he set out, with a gypsy lad as his guide, to find out for himself exactly how great the danger was, but though he travelled for miles in an ever widening circle from Twyning Green, he found nowhere that news of the hunt had not reached. By the time he returned to the camp, after an absence of several days, he was convinced that the only safe course was to lie low until the sensation caused by Francis Aldon's death and the escape of his supposed murderess had had time to die down.

As soon as he appeared, Bronwen came flying into

his arms, no longer the remote and mysterious elf-queen but an eager, loving woman of very human passion. She clung to him, sobbing with relief and gladness.

"Thanks be to God that you have returned! I have died a hundred deaths, thinking you dead or captured."

He caught her in a hard embrace, looking down at her with a light in his eyes which belied the casual irony of his reply. "I am not so easily disposed of, sweetheart, and you should not have fretted on my account. I would have returned sooner, but I had to learn the full extent of our danger."

Her eyes searched his face. "Is it very great?"

"Aldon has drawn the net even tighter than I expected, but we shall escape it yet. I think I see how it can be done, but first I must take counsel with the leader of this company. Come with me to seek him."

Benedict's plan was simple. It was that they should stay with the gypsies, travelling with them wherever they went, until either the search was less earnestly pursued or they had passed beyond the range of it. The Romany chief made no difficulty about this, for he was more than willing to do something which would avenge his people for being driven forth from one of the few places where they might camp unmolested, under the protection of the landowner. For many years, Aldon land had offered them sanctuary; now they had been dispossessed of their haven, just as Bronwen had been dispossessed, and all of them were eager for vengeance.

For Bronwen herself, in spite of the inevitable hardships of gypsy life, it was a magical time, those mellow, golden weeks of summer's dying. A time in which there was no past and no future, but only the enchanted present, and a happiness such as she had never known. She did not regret the choice made that night in the ruined chapel. Hers was a nature—inherited, perhaps, from her unknown mother—to love but once in her life, and that recklessly, completely; she had seen then, with an inner awareness which owed nothing to reason or logic, that here was her destiny. Now her love for Benedict possessed her utterly, heart and mind and body. She could scarcely remember the time when he was not a part of her life; or, if she did remember, it was a memory of emptiness, of desolation, of a loneliness which she only recognised now, in retrospect. The disasters which had engulfed her no longer mattered, for they had been no more than a necessary prelude to her meeting with him.

He, for his part, was content, for the many vicissitudes of his life had made it easy for him to accept events as they occurred. The considerations which had led him to embark upon a homeward journey were not forgotten, but the matter was not one of great urgency. He would resume the journey one day, but meanwhile there was a vagabond life which exactly suited his temperament; a spice of danger to give it savour; and Bronwen. Above all, there was Bronwen. Her strange, elusive beauty had ensnared him as completely as though she were indeed the witch they believed her to be, and he knew that even if they were destined to share no more than this brief spell of roving, he would never forget her. Bronwen, the enchantress, the elf-queen.

The gypsies, once they left their camp in the forest,

roamed from place to place, sometimes remaining in the same spot for no more than one night, sometimes for several. They were outcasts, welcome nowhere; distrusted, yet feared; a people with the curse of Cain upon them, doomed to wander for ever. Benedict, moving among them, lean, swarthy, dark of hair and eyes, might have been one of themselves, but for Bronwen complete disguise was less easy to achieve. The women had urged her to stain her white skin with walnut juice, but the thought repelled her, and when Benedict was appealed to, he flatly forbade it, saying that no matter how dark she made her complexion, the colour of her eyes would still betray her. So when the need arose she simply drew her shawl close about her face and hid her hands and arms within it, and if any stranger noticed this, they assumed that she was in some way disfigured.

It was an interlude which could not last for long. The day came when Benedict, emerging from their tent in the early morning, became aware of a sharpness in the air, the first tints of autumn on the trees, and knew that the time was fast approaching when they must abandon this roving life. Bronwen had so far endured the hardships of it without hurt, but she had been too softly reared to continue to face them once the summer was over.

That day he set off again to try to find out if the search for them had been abandoned. Since they were now some way to the west of Twyning Green, he hoped that this was sufficiently far from the influence of the Aldon family for the affair to have faded from people's minds, and he found the hope justified. It might not be prudent to linger in any of the neighbouring villages, but he did not think there would be any risk in passing through them.

When evening came, he took Bronwen a little apart from the rest of the company, up out of the hollow where the camp had been pitched, and told her that the time had come for them to part from their gypsy friends. She made no protest, but he saw a wistful look in her eyes.

"Where shall we go, Benedict?"

"To London," he said decisively, "whence I had come when we met. I have a lodging there to which I can take you, where I left my servant and the rest of my gear."

She looked startled. "I did not know that you had a servant."

"Did you suppose that my possessions amount to no more than I carry with me?" he countered with some amusement. "Yusuf—or Joseph, as I call him now that we are in England—came with me out of Barbary. I left him in London because he had been ailing, and because, not knowing what welcome I would receive from my uncle, it seemed pointless to take him on what might prove to be a fruitless journey."

"When must we go?"

He shrugged. "Tomorrow or the next day. There is nothing to be gained by delay. I will bargain with our friends for a mount for you, and if we set out betimes we should reach London by nightfall."

Bronwen nodded, but sighed, too, as she looked down the slope to the camp; at the dark humps of the tents between the trees, the fires blooming like bright flowers in the blue dusk.

"We have been happy, Benedict, have we not?"

His arm tightened around her. "Aye, sweeting, and shall be happier yet," he said gently. "A vagabond's life is well enough in summer, but it soon loses its savour when frost bites shrewdly, and wind and rain strip the forest bare. When winter comes you will be glad of a stout roof and a hearth-fire in place of a gypsy tent."

Remembering the misgiving with which she had contemplated a winter in the witch's cottage, she knew that he was right. Then the future had seemed bleak indeed, and now she was assured of shelter and protection—but for how long? How long before the trumpets of adventure sounded again in his ears, calling him away from the home and hearth-fire of which he spoke? She knew, better than he knew it himself, that the bonds of domesticity would soon begin to irk him; knew it and accepted it; that was the penalty of loving such a man as Benedict Forde.

They said farewell to the gypsies at sunrise two days later. Benedict had resumed his finery of lace and velvet, and Bronwen was dressed in the best the women could provide, with Benedict's silk-lined cloak over all, and her black hair coiled up into as fashionable a style as she could contrive. This would have to serve until London was reached. She was mounted on a handsome white pony purchased from the gypsy leader, and if its saddle and harness were shabby this was not likely to cause remark.

Riding at first by unfrequented ways, they found themselves by midday on the London road. Here they began to encounter other travellers, but no one paid any undue heed to them, and when they reached a village with a respectable-looking inn, Benedict decided that it would be safe to halt and dine. They dismounted, handed over the horses to an ostler who was lounging at the stable-door, and went into the house.

A narrow passage traversed it from front to back, and from beyond a door which stood ajar on their right issued a murmur of voices, dominated by the loud, confident tones of a man who was clearly in no doubt of his own importance.

Benedict went towards the door, and was actually reaching out to thrust it wide when he became aware of the convulsive clutch of Bronwen's hand on his arm. He checked, and glanced down at her to find her stricken, her eyes dilated, her face so white that even the lips were drained of colour, and unable to frame the words she was clearly trying to utter. At last, in a strangled whisper, she succeeded.

"I know that voice! Know it? Merciful God, could I ever forget it? It is Thomas Barnes, Sir John Aldon's servant."

. . . . .

Benedict swore softly and stepped back, frowning. "Are you certain?"

"Certain as death! Oh, Benedict, come away! Sir John himself may be here also."

"If he is, he will not be in the common tap-room." He laid his hand reassuringly over hers where it still clutched his sleeve. "Peace, sweetheart! I must see this

91

man Barnes, for it is always well to know the face of one's enemy."

He moved forward a pace and very gently pushed the door a few inches wider, until the self-important speaker came into view, seated at the end of a long, stained table. Benedict saw a big man, beginning to run to fat but nonetheless powerful, with a broad, florid face adorned by a fiercely upturned moustache and a tuft of beard. He held a pewter tankard brimming with ale in one hand, and was using the other to emphasise with flourishing gestures the bombastic speech he was addressing to a group of admiring rustics. Benedict caught a reference to recent events in London, and concluded from this that Barnes was returning from the capital rather than journeying towards it. That, at least, was a measure of good fortune.

A footstep sounded in the passage behind them. Bronwen gave a little gasp of fright, and Benedict turned to see an angular, grey-haired woman who was obviously the mistress of the house. She eyed them with a hint of suspicion, but asked civilly enough if she might serve them.

"You may, indeed," he replied easily. "We travel towards London, but my wife is not strong and the journey has exhausted her. I would have her rest for a while, but your room yonder is full of company."

The charm of his voice, combined as it was with easy assurance and a sombre richness of dress, was not without its effect, while Bronwen's white face and obvious distress served to confirm his words. The woman forgot suspicion and became sympathetic.

"To be sure, sir, the tap-room's no place for your

lady. There's a loud-voiced stranger there—well, only hark to him—and enough fools willing to drink his ale and listen to his boasts to keep him there for hours. Come you with me."

"I—I would be private," Bronwen said faintly, terrified that she was about to be ushered into some parlour, and the presence of Sir John Aldon.

"And so you shall, my dear. My best bedchamber be empty and ready, and you may rest there as quiet as can be."

She led them along the passage and up a twisting stair to a room with a dormer window looking out upon the village street. There was a big four-poster there, and she insisted that Bronwen should take off her cloak and shoes and lie down upon it. The shabbiness of the girl's dress brought a trace of the earlier suspicion into her eyes again, and her sharp glance went quickly to Bronwen's ringless left hand, but though she pursed her lips and looked reprovingly at Benedict, she made no comment, merely saying that she would fetch a cordial of her own brewing which would restore the young lady.

As soon as she had left the room Bronwen sprang up from the bed. "Benedict, what are we to do?"

"Why, nothing, sweetheart! No one has seen you save the inn-keeper's wife, and she has no reason to connect you with that braggart below. You will rest quietly here, as she bids you, and show proper gratitude for her kind care."

She eyed him with misgiving. "And you?"

The habitual irony of his expression deepened a little. "I go to make the acquaintance of Master

Barnes, and to discover if possible the purpose of his journey."

"Benedict, no!" she exclaimed in horror. "He saw you that day, and will surely recognise you."

"He saw me for a moment only, in a bad light, at a time when all his attention was upon you. He will not know me again."

"But if he does?" she insisted desperately. "This is to gamble with your life, and for what?"

"For the chance of learning what further measures Sir John has taken to apprehend us—if, indeed, he has taken any at all beyond those we already know. Fortune has led us to this house at the same time as Barnes, and I have learned never to turn my back upon Fortune's favours." He took her face gently between his hands and kissed her lips and smiled into her anxious eyes. "Play your part here, my love, and do not fear for me."

She clung to him as he kissed her, winding her arms about him as though to keep him forcibly at her side, but released him almost at once, knowing that only by never seeking to impose bonds upon him could she bind him to her. He kissed her again, swiftly and lightly this time, his thoughts already ranging ahead to the encounter with Thomas Barnes, then put her from him and went out, and she heard his firm, confident step going down the winding stair.

The next hour seemed endless. The inn-keeper's wife returned, and Bronwen forced herself to lie quietly on the bed until the woman left her again, even though every screaming nerve rebelled against such stillness. Her ears were strained to catch each sound from below, and she dreaded each moment to hear the uproar which would tell her that Benedict's identity had been discovered.

At last she heard him coming back, and knew from his face, the moment he entered the room, that he accounted the risk he had taken well worth while. In answer to her anxious, low-voiced question he said softly:

"Barnes has been to London on a matter of business between Aldon and his brother, the Colonel. To hear him speak of it, one would imagine Giles Aldon second in importance only to Cromwell himself, and Sir John the greatest land-owner in all England. Affairs of state could not invest Barnes, in his own eyes, with greater importance."

Bronwen frowned. "It is true that Sir John places great trust in him, and always employs him when there are confidential letters to be carried to the Colonel. He has been in their service for many years."

"He would have had me believe that neither could contrive without him, but for all that, I think poorly of their judgment. The fellow's a fool! He has bragged so much of the value of the packet of documents he carries that he almost invites its theft."

"Is he still below?"

"If he is, it is for a few minutes only, for he was already calling for his horse when I parted from him." Benedict went to the window. "Aye, yonder he rides! Come, sweetheart! Time for us to begone also."

"Do we not stay to dine?"

"At the next village, I promise you. There is a certain matter I must deal with first, and time presses."

He picked up the cloak as he spoke, and wrapped it

about her as he drew her with him to the door, so that her other questions died unspoken. She knew it would be useless to ask them. A subtle change had come over him, as though he had heard some call to arms inaudible to other ears, and she was no longer foremost in his thoughts.

He led her downstairs again, called for their horses and paid the shot. The inn-keeper's wife came with anxious inquiries, and Bronwen, without knowing why, rose to the occasion and assured her that all was well. They rode out of the village at an easy pace, but once the last houses were out of sight Benedict quickened this to a brisk trot, looking about him as though in search of something.

After about half a mile he appeared to find it, and turned aside to a sizable spinney a short distance from the road. Beneath the trees it was thick with undergrowth and they were obliged to skirt it for a minute or two before finding a way in, but when at length they had thrust their way into the heart of it they were completely hidden from any chance passer-by. Benedict looked about him with satisfaction.

"Yes, this will serve. Come, love, light down. I must leave you here for a while, but you are well hidden and no one will trouble you."

"Leave me?" She stared at him in dismay. "Why? Where are you going?"

"To pursue my acquaintance with Thomas Barnes." Benedict, already dismounted, reached up to swing her from the saddle, paying no heed to her gasp of protest. "I cannot stay now to tell you what I intend, but trust me. I will return before long."

"Benedict, for the love of God!" She clung desperately to him, clutching at his doublet with frantic fingers. "This is madness! We have evaded him—let well alone! Ride on to London."

"When I have done what is to do," he replied sternly, "and of what that is, I alone will be the judge. Loose me, Bronwen! You waste time, and I am in haste." When she did not immediately obey he grasped her wrists and with restrained impatience freed himself whether she would or no. Still holding her, he said again: "Trust me! I will return in a little while."

He put her from him, seized his horse's bridle and plunged again into the undergrowth. The white pony started to follow, and by the time Bronwen had checked it and tethered it to a tree, Benedict was out of sight, leaving her a prey to the most acute anxiety. Had she known exactly what he meant to do it would have been easier to bear, but, lacking such certain knowledge, she could only guess, her imagination painting pictures which grew steadily more alarming as time went by.

How long she waited in the spinney she did not know; it seemed an eternity. It was very quiet there, and warm despite the shade, for the tangle of trees and undergrowth shielded her from any breeze. Now and then she heard, very faintly, the sound of voices, or horses' hooves, or creaking wheels from the direction of the road, or the lowing of cattle and bleating of sheep from the meadows, but otherwise only the hum of insects and the occasional call and flutter of a bird disturbed the silence. She spread her cloak on the ground beneath a tree and sat on it, leaning back against the trunk, but was too uneasy to be still for long.

The shadows were beginning to lengthen when at last he returned, and Bronwen had passed through every stage of anxiety from irritation to despair, so that when he thrust through the spinney to her side she forgot all the reproaches and cutting rebukes she had been rehearsing, and simply went into his arms and held him very tightly, not speaking, trembling with the intensity of her relief.

"Why, sweeting, what's this?" he teased her gently. "Did I not promise to return?"

She nodded, her face hidden against his chest, her voice was muffled. "Yes, but I did not know where you had gone, what mischance might have befallen you. Oh, my love, never treat me so again! Trust me, as I have trusted you."

"Be sure I trust you." He held her off from him a little to look down into her eyes; his tone was serious. "It was lack of time, not lack of trust, which took me away in such haste. I had in mind a certain spot on the road where I wished to come up with Barnes—or rather, that I hoped to reach before him."

She looked searchingly at him. "And did you?"

"Aye, by cutting across country. It was a stretch of woodland, very dense and thick, with the road no more than a tunnel through it. We passed that way earlier, and I marked it then as a meet place for an ambush." He smiled grimly, and drew from the breast of his doublet a packed of papers, tied about with thin silk cord and bearing the name and title of Sir John Aldon. "I was right."

Bronwen stared at the packet. "You took those from Barnes? Benedict, why?"

"So that I might learn their content. If Barnes was to be believed they are of great import, and the time might come when it would be useful to have some weapon against Aldon and his brother. I thought the papers might treat of some secret matter they would be reluctant to have revealed."

"And do they? Have you examined them?"

"I have, and they do not. A simple matter of business only, though the letter Giles Aldon sends with him holds some interest for you and me. It seems he arrived at Twyning Hall on the day after young Francis's death, and it is he whom we have to blame for the thoroughness of the search for us. Then affairs demanded his return to London—a stroke of good fortune for us, I fancy—and his brother has now sent him word of the failure of the hunt." He chuckled. "Sir John, it seems, is beginning to believe that I am no mortal man, but the Colonel will have none of it. If we have not been found, he writes, it is because the search was not pursued with sufficient diligence."

Bronwen was looking at him with perplexity and dismay. "But this profits us not at all, and now you have waylaid Thomas Barnes and the hunt will be up again. Oh, why would you not heed what I said, and let well alone?"

A flicker of annoyance crossed his face. "I do not order matters quite so ill. Barnes never saw who attacked him, for I had hidden myself in the branches of a great tree above the road and dropped down upon him as he rode beneath. The fall stunned him."

"And when he regains his senses? What then?"

"He will find himself in the depths of the wood, lacking both horse and boots. The beast I led for some way before turning it loose, the boots I weighted with stones and heaved into the first duck-pond I passed. By the time Barnes succeeds in raising the alarm, we shall be nearing London."

She allowed herself to be mollified, and even to take some satisfaction in the thought of Barnes's discomfiture, but said with lingering severity:

"I grant you, then, that no harm has been done, but no good either, for all the delay and the risk." She paused, looking suspiciously at him, seeing a gleam of amusement in his eyes. "Or is there yet more to tell?"

"There is indeed. I condemned Barnes for a fool, for bragging so much about the value of those papers, but I did him less than justice. By making so much of them he led his hearers to suppose he carried nothing else." He turned towards his horse to thrust his hand into one of the saddle-bags, adding shamelessly: "You may give thanks, sweetheart, that I am experienced in the business of plundering, or, having secured the papers, I might have searched no farther. As it is . . ."

He left the sentence unfinished, turning to her again holding a small leather bag. Loosening the string which secured it, he took her hand and tipped some of the contents into her palm. Bronwen saw the gleam of gold coins, and gasped. "Aldon gold," Benedict remarked with grim satisfaction. "Barnes carried four such bags—by my reckoning, close upon five hundred pounds. Little enough, no doubt, compared with that which your foster-father bequeathed to you, but something, at least, salvaged from the ruin of his wishes and your rights."

She lifted troubled eyes to his. "Yet—stolen gold, Benedict. Oh, my love, I am not judging you, but have we the right . . .?"

"Had they the right to rob you and drive you forth and seek your death? To use the law to flout their kinsman's wishes? Had I taken ten times the amount it would have been no more than your due. Yours, Bronwen, whom Sir Edwin cherished as a daughter from the day of your birth."

"Yes, that is true," she said slowly. "He intended me to be provided for." Then she shook her head. "I cannot! To take it thus, like a thief, would make me as base as they."

She broke off then, seeing his face, realising that in her uncertainty and distress she had said a thing more wounding to him than she would ever have said in anger, with intent to hurt. "Stolen gold—a thief." This to a man who by his own confession had for years lived by plunder; a man whom she loved with her whole heart and being, and, loving thus, had neither remembered nor cared what his life had been.

"Benedict," she whispered. "Love, do not look at me so. I did not mean to say that."

"Not to say it—that I can believe." His voice was ice and death, bleak with the hurt she had dealt him. "But sometimes that which is in the thoughts slips out through the lips before we are aware of it. If Aldon's kin are base, who rob by due process of the law, what then am I?"

"I did not mean it so!" She was almost weeping

now. "I had forgotten what you told me of your past deeds, for it matters nothing to me. Less than nothing. I love you."

"Aye, so you have told me, times enough. What you have not told me, until now, is that you despise me as a thief."

"I do not despise you. Love takes no account of such things." She saw the continuing disbelief in his eyes and drew herself up, facing him with pride, with anger, with desperate entreaty. "Benedict, this is to insult me. Do you think I would have become the mistress of a man I despised?"

"I think," he said, "that you had no choice. That night we met, you were desperate for a protector, and you had seen that I was capable of protecting you. You saw, too, that there was one sure way of winning my protection. But the next day, when we spoke of my past life, you learned that you had given yourself to an escaped slave, a heathen pirate—in short, to a thief. And for that, you cannot forgive me."

"If that were so," she said proudly, "I would have parted from you."

"Would you? With the witch-hunt still baying at your heels? No, you knew there was no going back, but, being a woman, and gently reared, for your pride's sake you had to try to convince me—and yourself too, for aught I know—that you surrendered yourself for love, and not expediency."

"It is the truth," she said sadly, "and I did convince you of it, did I not?"

He shrugged. "I wanted you," he said brutally. "I think that while I draw breath I shall never cease to want you, despise me as you will." He thrust the gold out of sight again in the saddle-bag, then bent to pick up her cloak from the ground. "Now come, or we shall find ourselves benighted on the road."

She looked blankly at him. "Is that all you are going to say?"

"What more is there to say?" He flung the cloak about her, gripping its two ends close about her throat and holding her prisoner to look down with grim mockery into her face. "I still desire you, and you are still dependent upon me. We have had the truth laid bare between us, Bronwen, but nothing has changed."

●   ●   ●   ●   ●   ●

Nothing had changed. Nothing—and everything. Both of them knew it, and neither would admit it. They kept to the plans they had made. Rode on to London. Came at nightfall to Benedict's lodging near Cheapside, where his servant, a slim, dark-eyed, olive-skinned young man, greeted his master with relief, and accepted Bronwen's presence respectfully and with a complete lack of curiosity.

Joseph, the son of an English seaman and an Arab mother, had been in Benedict's service since he was a boy and was, Bronwen discovered, whole-heartedly devoted to his interests. He spoke perfect English and wore English clothes, but there was still something alien about his aquiline face with its dark eyes and neat black beard, his silent, cat-like movements and the profound and quite genuine veneration with which he regarded his master. These things set him apart from his sturdily independent English counterparts. He was looked at askance, and, even in the short time he had dwelt there, had become a figure of some note in the neighbourhood.

This, Bronwen decided, was of a piece with everything else about Benedict Forde, who, without making the smallest attempt to do so, attracted attention wherever he went. His height and his gaunt, forbidding face; the sombre richness of his dress; above all, a self-assurance so complete that it had no need of swagger or bluster, made him a conspicuous figure even in crowded city streets. Men instinctively drew aside to let him pass, resenting their own impulse even as they yielded to it, and women looked at him with more than fleeting interest. He went his indifferent way, paying as little heed to the one as to the other.

Bronwen, observing this, yet failed to see how completely she, too, fitted into the picture. At first, after one excursion to buy materials and engage a seamstress, she stayed indoors, too proud to walk the London streets in her shabby gypsy dress, but as soon as her new clothes were ready she ended this self-imposed confinement. She had chosen the rich stuffs and strong, brilliant colours she loved, and had the gowns fashioned with no regard for the sober restraint in dress which, though not always practised, was generally held to be the ideal of Cromwellian London. With her fine clothes and unusual looks she turned as many heads as Benedict himself, and if their neighbours regarded them with disapproval, this was tinged with an odd kind of satisfaction. It was only to be expected,

104

those worthy folk agreed, that the imposing Mr. Forde would acquire so striking a mistress.

The gold stolen from Thomas Barnes had been securely hidden away, and neither Benedict nor Bronwen referred to it again, but the thought of it, and of the quarrel it had provoked, lay like a drawn sword between them. The things they had said to each other that day had struck deep, and though, on the surface, everything was now as it had been before, it was as though a wound had healed over and left poison festering beneath the skin.

At first it was possible to disguise the gulf between them by occupying themselves with their surroundings, for Benedict was more familiar with foreign cities than with London, and Bronwen with no city at all. There was plenty to see, even though London under the "rule of the saints" lacked much of its one-time gaiety and colour. The pageantry of the Court was but a memory, the theatres were closed and many of the old sports and pastimes forbidden, but there was still the mighty fortress of the Tower; the river, London's great highway, crowded with craft of all descriptions; London Bridge with its twin rows of houses, its twenty narrow arches through which the water rushed like a mill-race, and the heads of traitors rotting on pikes above one end; St Paul's Cathedral and the Royal Exchange; the palaces of Whitehall and St James's.

The time came, however, when these diversions began to pall, and as this happened the tension between Bronwen and Benedict steadily mounted. They quarrelled repeatedly, and though each quarrel was followed by a passionate reconciliation, peace never endured for long. Their differences were all over trivial matters and the true, underlying cause was never mentioned, but both knew well enough where the source of the trouble lay. Each quarrel was a little more bitter than the last, and a little slower to heal.

It was this constant bickering, more than anything else, which drove Benedict to the decision he reached early in October. It followed hard on the heels of a particularly sharp disagreement with Bronwen, which sent him stalking furiously from the house to stride through the narrow streets with so grim an expression on his face that more than one person stepped hastily out of his way. He found himself at length by the river, at one of the many landing-stages where scarlet-coated watermen plied for hire, and standing there, staring at the broad stream dotted with swans and crowded with busy craft, he came to the conclusion that the present situation was no longer to be borne. Bronwen was in no danger now. It seemed an apt moment to resume his interrupted journey to Suffolk.

Characteristically, he resolved to set out with the least possible delay, but when he reached home he found the place empty. There was no reason at all why Bronwen should have sat there waiting for him, yet he felt irrationally annoyed that she had not. As evening drew on, however, annoyance began to be tinged with disquiet, for though she had obviously taken Joseph to escort her, as Benedict had told her she must always do if she went out without him, so prolonged an absence was unusual. Against his will, he began to picture the various mischances which might have occurred, and had almost reached the point of setting out in search of her when he heard her footstep on the stairs leading to their rooms. A moment later she entered and paused just within the door, blinking a little in the candle-light, for outside it was now almost dark.

"Oh, you are here!" she exclaimed. "I did not think you would return so soon."

She did not seem particularly pleased to see him, but apart from that there was nothing more than mild surprise in her voice. Benedict, however, already in a bad mood and with his anxiety on her behalf illogically transformed into resentment, chose to read dismay into it as well. Studying her from beneath scowling brows, he said unpleasantly:

"Does my presence inconvenience you? Did you pick a quarrel just to rid yourself of my company?"

Bronwen gasped. "*I* pick a quarrel? To the best of my recollection, it was of your making."

They glared at each other. Joseph, who had followed Bronwen into the room, put down a package he was carrying, bowed silently to his master and went softly away to his own quarters. Bronwen came farther into the room, loosened her cloak of fine crimson cloth and dropped it across a stool; the rose-coloured satin of her gown shimmered in the candle-light.

Morosely Benedict continued to study her, angry with her for causing him needless anxiety, and with himself because, in spite of their quarrels, the prospect of parting from her was suddenly far less acceptable than it had seemed when he made the decision.

"Where the devil have you been until this hour?" he demanded irritably.

For a few seconds she looked at him, and he thought she was not going to reply. Then she shrugged slightly, as though deciding to humour him.

"At the Royal Exchange. I went to choose the silk for a new gown."

"A whole afternoon to choose a length of silk?"

"That was done in less than an hour." Bronwen's own temper was rising, and she spoke impatiently. "I find it more amusing, however, to stroll around the Royal Exchange than to sit alone at home."

He had no reason, apart from his own ill-humour, to disbelieve her. In all London, no place fascinated her as much as the Exchange, that meeting-place of merchants, with its fine shops, its throngs of people, its air of being the pulsing heart of a great and prosperous city. To it came the wealthy to purchase gold or silver plate and rare glass; their wives and daughters to choose silks and satins and jewels; gallants to keep assignations with those same wives and daughters. There was a constant coming and going of coaches, and of lackeys who idled over the errands they had been sent upon, or gossiped as they waited for master or mistress. The week before, however, when Bronwen and Benedict had happened to become separated in the crowd, a young gentleman had tried to strike up an acquaintance with her, until he realised that she was not, after all, unescorted. Benedict, recalling the incident, now chose to refer obliquely to it.

"No doubt you find it particularly amusing when you have only Joseph to escort you."

Bronwen, who had turned towards the fire, spun

round again to face him, her eyes blazing. "What do you mean by that?"

"I mean that though Joseph is more than competent to protect you, he is still no more than a servant, and would have no choice but to obey you if you found reason to send him away for a while."

"I am relieved to hear it," she retorted. "I thought you had set him to keep watch over me whether I would or no. That is the custom of Islam, is it not?"

"In Islam," he replied grimly, "you would not set foot outside the women's quarters. Or, if it became necessary for you to do so, you would be veiled from head to toe. Truly, the Muslim way with women has much to recommend it."

"And the ways of men are the same the world over, but remember that I am not one of your Barbary slave-girls."

"More's the pity! At least they were never shrews."

There was a pause. In that pleasant room, bright with fire-flicker and candle-glow, they confronted each other like strangers, like mortal enemies; as though there had never been two lovers who roamed the summer forest, absorbed in each other despite the shadow of danger hovering near them. Now summer had gone, and the danger with it; and gone, too, it seemed, was the magic of those enchanted days and nights. The prosaic world of the city had caught them up, hedged them about with commonplace things which bounded their life within narrow confines to which neither was accustomed—for though Bronwen had lived all her days at Twyning Hall, her mind had ranged far on the wings of the learning she had had of her foster-father.

They both fretted against the change without being fully aware of what ailed them, and it was this, as much as the original bitter quarrel, which sowed discord between them.

"Since you find me so shrewish, and since I have no claim upon you," Bronwen said icily at last, "I marvel that you do not abandon me for a woman more to your taste. Or do you imagine that one day, out of gratitude, I shall learn to abase myself to your every whim, as humbly as though I had indeed been purchased in the slave-market?"

"No," he sneered, "I do not look for miracles. It is true, though, that I have had my fill of shrewishness. I leave London in the morning."

The colour drained from her face. "You are leaving me?"

"No need for such dismay, my love," he said mockingly. "I am leaving you, but not unprovided for. Joseph will remain, and sufficient funds to maintain the household until I return."

"You intend, then, to return?" There was still a slight tremor in Bronwen's voice, but she contrived to match irony with irony. "Is it permitted to inquire where you are going?"

"Where else but to Monksfield, my uncle's house in Suffolk? You know why I was going there, and that purpose remains unaltered. Indeed, it becomes a necessity. We have not stinted ourselves since we came to London, and my small resources will not last for ever."

She flushed, glancing briefly towards the package that Joseph had carried home for her. "You should have warned me to be thrifty. I was not bred to it, and did not realise the need."

A sense of having been put in the wrong had made her speak haughtily, and Benedict's lean cheeks darkened with annoyance. He said curtly:

"There *is* no need as yet, nor will be if I can replenish my purse, and the only chance of doing that honestly lies at Monksfield. If I fail there, I will have no choice but to return to the only trade at which I am truly proficient."

"You would go seafaring again?" There was a hint of breathlessness now in Bronwen's voice. "That is what you mean, is it not?"

He leaned back against the edge of the table, arms folded, and sardonically regarded her. In the candlelight his gaunt, dark face was a very mask of mockery, and mockery sounded, too, in the deep, compelling tones of his voice.

"You know it is not. The trade I follow has this advantage—it can be practised as well on land as at sea. I have weapons and a good horse. It is enough." The mockery deepened, became bitter, almost savage in its intensity. "How say you, Bronwen? Would it irk your pride and your tender conscience to be a highwayman's doxy?"

So that was the direction his thoughts were taking. She knew he would not hesitate to follow that hazardous course if all else failed, but the dismay she felt had nothing to do with conscience or with pride. Only with fear for him. She remembered their journey to London, and the roadside gibbets where the shrivelled corpses of highway robbers swung in chains as a grim warning to other wrongdoers, and dread touched her with an icy breath which seemed to numb wits and voice alike.

Benedict, misunderstanding her silence, and the frozen stillness with which she was looking at him, read into it only anger and disdain. The sneer on his lips became more pronounced.

"But I already know the answer to that, do I not? If you will not take what is yours by right, because it comes to you soiled by the hands of a thief, how much less willing would you be to live upon gold stolen from strangers." He laughed, a quiet chuckle mirthless as hell itself. "An accommodating conscience, upon my life, which scorns the thief yet permits you still to take him as your lover!"

It was the first time any reference had been made to the original cause of their estrangement, and it betrayed, had Bronwen paused to consider it, how deep his hurt had gone; but she did not pause. It was not only Benedict who had been hurt that day beside the London road.

"I still need your protection, as you have not been slow to remind me. What choice have I but to purchase it by the only means at my command?"

For a moment she thought that she had gone too far, for he took a pace towards her and murder glared at her out of the dark eyes. She faced him defiantly, dissembling a sudden stab of alarm, and after a second or two he cursed deeply in a foreign tongue, then turned sharp on his heel and strode out of the room. The door slammed shut behind him, and a minute later she heard the sound echoed by the crash of the heavier door leading to the street. For a little while she remained standing rigidly where he had left her, and then she dropped into a chair and covered her face with her hands.

This time there was no reconciliation. They lay apart that night, and in the morning took leave of each other with stiff formality, speaking only of practical matters, and that as briefly as possible. Joseph, fetching the black horse to the door, observed with misgiving that his master's face was as forbidding as a gaunt mask hammered out of bronze, the dark eyes sombre beneath the heavy brows.

When the servant went back to the room upstairs, he found Bronwen sitting by the fire. Her hands lay passive along the arms of her chair, her head rested against its high, carved back, and her face was white and still, drained of all emotion. It was only when he drew nearer that he saw the tears running unchecked down her cheeks.

Part Five

Benedict brought his horse to a halt beneath a towering beech-tree and sat looking across a quarter of a mile of rough parkland at the manor-house of Monksfield, home of the Forde family for generations. Above him the branches tossed and thrummed in a cold wind sweeping in from the North Sea a score of miles away; a wind that plucked at his cloak and rippled the scarlet plume in his hat and stripped the beech-tree ruthlessly of its leaves. They spun through the air all about him, and whirled and scurried across the grass, bright as plundered gold from a broken treasure-chest. A good omen, perhaps? He accorded the thought the mockery of a fleeting smile as he studied the distant house.

It seemed not to have changed at all in twenty years, but still stood, mellow in the mellow autumn sunshine, solid, prosperous and enduring. Its windows glinted in the sunlight, smoke rose from its tall, twisted chimneys and was whirled away into nothingness by the boisterous wind. To the right he could see the gleam of water against an ancient stone wall—for Monksfield had been moated once—and between it and the beech-tree a small herd of deer grazed, peaceful beneath the blue October sky.

Benedict touched spur to his horse and rode on towards the house, and as he approached the deer, an old stag raised its stately, antlered head. Then, as though at a word of command, the whole herd stopped feeding and broke away, with a flash of white tails and the drumming of small hooves on the grass, fleeing before the dark rider who came at a steady canter across the park. A gatehouse gave access to the courtyard around which the house was built, and Benedict passed straight through without a pause, paying no heed to the old gatekeeper who came hobbling out at his approach.

The sound of iron-shod hooves clattering beneath the echoing arch attracted the attention of a woman who sat sewing in the window above the big, square porch, which was, in fact, more like a tiny room, as big as the porch itself, with windows on three sides. She glanced down to see who came with such arrogant lack of ceremony, and as the rider emerged from the shadow of the gatehouse a gust of wind, whistling through the archway, snatched at his cloak and spread it wide like great wings. The woman caught her breath in a little gasp of fear, for, just for an instant, it seemed to her as though a gigantic bird of prey had alighted in the courtyard.

She frowned impatiently at her own fantasy, and

leaned forward a little to watch him dismount, then, as he passed out of sight beneath the porch, she laid aside her sewing and went softly down the two steps which led from her window to the gallery above the hall. Below her, to the left, she could see Sir Nicholas Forde sitting beside the fire, and, as she watched, a serving-man crossed the hall to answer an imperious knocking.

There was a murmur of voices, and then the visitor came round the carved screens between porch and hall, his spured boots making a faint, jingling sound on the flagstones. Looking down upon him, she could see only the top of the broad-brimmed, scarlet-plumed hat, the wide shoulders, and a long sword upthrust beneath the flowing cloak. She heard Sir Nicholas say heartily:

"Good-day to you, sir, and welcome to Monksfield. I think I do not know your name."

The stranger's voice replied. "Yet you should sir, for it is the same as your own. I am Benedict Forde."

It was a beautiful voice, deep and expressive, seeming to say so much more than the mere words it uttered, yet the woman who now heard it for the first time remained untouched by its magic. It could not efface the memory of that first glimpse she had had of him as he rode out from under the archway, or the sense of foreboding which had touched her then. A foreboding which disclosure of his identity served to increase.

In the hall, Sir Nicholas was staring open-mouthed at his visitor. "What's this you say? *Benedict* Forde? Young Benedict, who ran off a score of years ago? It is not possible!"

"Yet it is so, sir. Young no longer, I fear, so small

116

wonder you do not know me, but I *am* your nephew, Benedict."

Still Sir Nicholas stared at him, and Benedict read doubt in his eyes. He was prepared for this, for it was not likely that his uncle would accept at once, without question, the statement of his identity. He bore no resemblance now to the lanky, overgown boy who had fled fom Monksfield, and after twenty years, even the memory of that boy must have faded and grown dim.

"I do not ask you, sir, to accept my word," he said easily, "only to give me leave to prove to you that I speak the truth. There are many ways in which I might do so, but one, I think, will suffice. Do you recall an occasion when your son Richard and I, being then about ten years old, took antique weapons from the armoury and engaged in a mock battle which came near to costing me my life? The sword Dick had chosen was too heavy for him. It slipped, and struck me in the side of the neck." He removed his hat, and, stepping closer to the old man's chair, bent forward, pushing aside his long hair. "I bear that scar still. It may be that you recognise it."

For a few seconds Sir Nicholas stared at the long, puckered scar against the bronzed skin, and then he surged up out of his chair and gripped the younger man by the shoulders. Benedict could feel that he was trembling.

"You are he! As I live, you *are* my nephew! Lad, lad, we thought you dead years agone! Praise be to God that we were wrong."

He broke off, his face working, his eyes moist, the tightness of his grip on Benedict's shoulders conveying the depth of his emotion, but he was not a man easily to give way to his feelings. A moment later he was shouting for the servants.

"Ned! Walter! Bring wine—the best we have! And one of you send to find your mistress and bid her here. Miss Mercy, too! We have cause for rejoicing."

Benedict was gratified that he should think so. He had hoped for a welcome, in fact, he had depended on it, but not even his self-assurance had foreseen that he would be greeted like a returning prodigal. Sir Nicholas had always possessed strong family feeling, a patriarchal instinct which liked nothing better than to gather his kinfolk together under Monksfield's hospitable roof, but he, Benedict, was the black sheep, the renegade who had deliberately severed all family ties. It could not be as simple as this; just to ride up to the door to be welcomed with open arms. Both by nature and experience he was too cynical to believe in so easy a victory.

His uncle's next words, while telling him nothing he did not already know, offered at least a partial explanation of that welcome. Having despatched the servants on their various errands, and motioned him to a seat beside the fire, the old man said gravely:

"A cause for rejoicing, and yet for sorrowing also, that there are so few of your kindred left to welcome you home. Did you know, nephew, of the grievous losses our family has suffered?"

Benedict inclined his head. "I learned of them from Harry Kirke, whom I lately encountered in Paris. To be frank, sir, after I had talked with him I accounted it my duty to come home."

118

"Yes, poor Harry! He was misguided enough to embroil himself in Royalist conspiracy, and when the plot was discovered was obliged to go into exile to avoid the just consequences. It was a cruel blow to his parents, for they had already lost two sons in battle, but so it has been with us all. There can be scarcely a family in the land which has come unscathed through the wars."

He was silent for a moment or two, sadness in his face as he reflected on the toll death had taken of his own family during those years of bitter civil strife, but then he shook off the melancholy and looked across at this swarthy stranger who was yet a man of his own blood.

"The Lord has been merciful to me, His servant. I have grieved that the name of Forde must die with me, yet now you are restored to us, as though from the grave itself." A sudden thought seemed to strike him. "Are you wed, Benedict? Have you sons of your own?"

Benedict was tempted to reply, none that he knew of, but restrained an impulse which would do him no good in his uncle's eyes. The Fordes had always maintained a tradition of strict morality, and now he sensed something more, an atmosphere of religious fervour which, while lacking the fanaticism of the extreme Puritans, yet warned him to tread warily. The hapless Harry Kirke had told him that his brothers and cousins had fought in Cromwell's Ironside army; it would no doubt be prudent to conceal the fact that while they were offering up their lives in the name of the True Religion, their kinsman had commanded an Algerine pirate galley and professed himself, no matter with how little real conviction, one of the Faithful of Islam.

119

"I am not wed, sir," he replied quietly. "I have always been a rover, soldiering or seafaring, and in such life there is little place for wife or home or family."

"A pity, a pity!" Sir Nicholas shook his head. "Still, time enough to amend that. You are a young man yet. Ah, here comes Edith, my daughter-in-law. Poor Richard's widow, you understand, and now mistress of my house."

Benedict, rising, saw a slight woman in widow's weeds coming down the staircase at the far end of the hall. He watched her come towards him, seeing a pale face which might have been pretty once but now was thin and careworn, with bitterness and discontent in the line of the lips.

"Daughter," Sir Nicholas greeted her, "here is a matter of great wonder and joy to us all here at Monksfield. You have heard me speak of Benedict, my brother Benjamin's youngest son, who left us so many years ago. This is he."

Benedict bowed. Edith Forde inclined her head, unsmiling, and kept her thin hands folded before her, making no attempt to extend one of them in welcome. Benedict, coming erect again, looking down into cold, hostile blue eyes, and knew that here was one person who would never rejoice at his return. This was the difficulty his cynicism had foreseen, the obstacle in the way of achieving his purpose.

"Mrs Forde is rendered dumb," he murmured, and knew from the flicker of anger in her eyes that his mockery had struck home. "I crave your pardon, madam, for this abrupt arrival. It would have been better, perhaps, to have sent word of my coming."

"Nonsense, nonsense!" Sir Nicholas retorted briskly. "We are all amazed, it is true, but good tidings are ever welcome. Edith, where is Mercy? I told the servants to summon her here."

"She will come directly," Mrs Forde replied. "Martin Warner has brought her the spaniel pup he promised, and nothing would content her but to take the little creature out to play. She should be usefully employed indoors, but there! She will pay no heed to me. She has been too much indulged."

"Peace, daughter! Mercy is but sixteen, and already has seen too much of sorrow. Let her be merry while she may. Come, pour the wine. We will not stay for her."

A servant had set wine and glasses on the table in the middle of the hall. Edith filled two, and carried one to Sir Nicholas and one to Benedict. The latter suspected that she would rather be handing him a cup of poison.

"You do not drink with us, madam?"

"I must beg you, sir, to hold me excused. Wine does not sit well with me."

There was a sound of footsteps and laughter, and a boy and a girl came round the screens towards them. He was a slim, fresh-faced youngster in good but sober clothes, she small of build, and plump with the plumpness of extreme youth. Fair curls, a little disordered, clustered about a pretty face whipped to rosy colour by the wind; blue eyes surprised and frankly curious, surveyed the tall stranger standing with her mother and grandfather. She carried a silky-coated puppy in her arms.

"My child," Sir Nicholas greeted her, "we have had glad news this day. This gentleman is your kinsman, Benedict Forde, returned home at last after many years. Nephew, my grand-daughter, Mercy."

Benedict bowed with as much formality as he had used towards Edith, and Mercy, in whose face surprise had deepened to blank amazement, dropped a flustered curtsy. The puppy, squirming in her arms, nuzzled eagerly at her cheek with small pink tongue; she giggled, then guiltily bit her lip, looking quickly at her mother and then back to Benedict's forbidding countenance. He saw that she looked apprehensive.

"And a glad surprise for me, sir," he said with a smile. "I have travelled the world over, but seldom have I seen a more charming picture than this which greets me here at home."

The words were simple, but his beautiful voice made of them a compliment which would have flattered a more experienced woman than Mercy.

She blushed and dimpled, saying shyly and rather breathlessly: "You are very welcome, sir. I am happy to make your acquaintance."

"And this," Sir Nicholas continued, indicating Mercy's companion, "is Martin Warner. His father, Colonel Warner, lately acquired Trapton Hall and so became our nearest neighbour."

Benedict acknowledged the introduction with a careless nod, and young Warner bowed stiffly, too inexperienced to disguise his instinctive suspicion and resentment of this assured stranger. The faintest of sardonic smiles touched Benedict's lips and he turned again to Mercy, making some idle remark about the

122

puppy, stretching out his hand to caress the little creature's silky ears.

Mercy responded readily to the praise of her new pet, and it was plain that she did not share her mother's and Martin's instant aversion to the newcomer. Benedict saw that Edith Forde was looking venomously at him, and he looked back with mocking indifference. Edith had chosen to make an enemy of him at the outset; she would learn that could be a dangerous thing to do.

     •   •   •   •   •

News of Benedict's return spread swiftly through the neighbourhood. Young Martin Warner carried it back with him to his home at nearby Trapton Hall; the house-servants at Monksfield passed it on to the farm-labourers and villagers; within twenty-four hours everyone knew that the squire's long-lost newphew had come home at last.

The young were frankly curious; their elders, those who remembered Benedict in his boyhood, were dubious as to whether or not his return would prove to be the blessing Sir Nicholas apparently considered it. It was recalled that Benedict Forde had ever been the ne'er-do-well of his family, the wild one, the rebel who had dared to defy duty and custom and abscond rather than yield to his father's will. It was not to be supposed that so intransigent a spirit had been humbled by twenty years' adventuring.

Sir Nicholas himself appeared to harbour no such doubts. He and Benedict sat talking far into the night, both of the latter's chequered career and of events in England, and, more particularly, at Monksfield during his long absence; and if Benedict learned rather more than he disclosed, his uncle was not aware of it. Sir Nicholas was by nature a direct and open man who did not look for deviousness in others; least of all in one of his own kin.

He spoke with quiet sorrow of the death, from smallpox, of Benedict's father and youngest sister; of his two brothers who had been killed during the wars; and of a second sister who had died, childless, after only two years of marriage.

The remaining sister was still living, but her husband had risen to some prominence in the Ironside army, and they no longer lived in Suffolk. Benedict listened with becoming solemnity and an almost total lack of any emotion. The only member of his family for whom he had felt deep affection was his mother, and she had died before he went away.

Of his own life he spoke with what seemed to be frankness but was not. He told of his imprisonment by the Spaniards but not of his adoption of the Catholic faith; of his rescue by Algerine pirates and of sailing with them, but left Sir Nicholas with the impression that this had been done reluctantly and for a short time only, until a way of escape occurred. Even so, the old man was troubled.

"So for a time, nephew, you lived among these barbarians and practised the abominations of their heathen faith. I fear that is a grave sin."

"Sir," Benedict replied bluntly, "I venture to believe that in such circumstances a man may be forgiven for

124

using the outward trappings of an alien religion if he does so with no true conviction."

"Perhaps, perhaps," Sir Nicholas agreed with a sigh. "It is not for me to sit in judgment upon you, for how can I tell if my own faith would be strong enough for me to accept slavery rather than deny my God? And such slavery!"

"Exactly!" Benedict agreed grimly. "There may be some men with the faith and the courage to exchange a Christian rowing-bench for a Muslim one, but I am not among them."

"I do not condemn you, my boy, but it will be as well not to noise the truth abroad. There are many who would hold it against you, and we want no unpleasantness to mar your homecoming."

Benedict shrugged. "As you wish, sir. I have learned how to keep my own counsel, and I have no wish to cause discord between you and your neighbours."

There was likely to be discord enough, he reflected beneath the roof of Monksfield itself if Edith persisted in her hostile attitude towards him. He assumed this to have its root in self-interest, since with his return and his uncle's reaction to it, Mercy could no longer be considered the sole and undisputed heiress of Monksfield, but though he could understand Edith's dismay, he was indifferent to it. He had come home in the hope and expectation of securing his future, and if Edith were not prepared to see him share the inheritance, she must take the consequences.

On the following day Sir Nicholas, who was still active and vigorous despite advancing years, desired Benedict to ride with him around the estate. Mercy went

125

with them, and though Sir Nicholas expressed surprise that her mother allowed her to neglect her household tasks, Benedict thought cynically that the reason was obvious. The girl clearly held a prime place in her grandfather's affections, and Edith had no intention of allowing this to be jeopardised by an interloper, nephew or no. If Benedict was to ride with Sir Nicholas, Mercy should go, too; and no doubt would be closely questioned on her return.

The estate of Monksfield, as he soon perceived, was prosperous, and larger than in his boyhood, Sir Nicholas having purchased a considerable acreage since the end of the wars. They rode past the modest house where Benedict had been born, and which, his uncle told him with a hint of apology, was now leased to a tenant. Benedict nodded indifferently. His old home meant nothing to him.

That was only one of numerous changes which had taken place. In the main, the eastern counties of England had stood for Parliament—Cromwell himself was a Cambridgeshire man—but there had been some who supported the King, and who now, defeated and ruined, had seen their lands pass into the hands of their victorious enemies. Thus had Sir Nicholas enlarged his estate, and his neighbour, Colonel Warner, come into possession of Trapton Hall.

Within two days of his homecoming, Benedict learned that the Colonel and his son must be numbered with Edith Forde among those who wished him no good. They came to Monksfield together, the Colonel on the pretext of discussing with Sir Nicholas a boundary dispute involving the two estates, Martin apparently for no other reason than to dance attendance upon Mercy.

Warner was a stern-faced, humorless man, very soberly dressed and with his hair cut short in the manner which had originally earned the Parliamentarians the nickname of "Roundheads." He looked with unconcealed disapproval at Benedict's velvet and lace and flowing curls, instinctively distrusting an elegance which seemed to him to indicate too great a concern with the follies of the world. A soldier himself, he recognised another fighting-man, but decided at once that such fighting was unlikely to have been done in the cause of righteousness.

"Your return to Monksfield, Mr Forde," he said severely when Benedict had been made known to him, "has brought your good uncle comfort in his latter years. His friends rejoice with him, that the Lord has been thus merciful."

"It is my hope, sir," Benedict replied with becoming gravity, "that they will never have cause to do otherwise."

"Say rather that it is your prayer," Warner admonished him sharply, "as it should be your prayer to be worthy of the Lord's grace, like your kinsmen who gave their lives in His cause. They fought and died for God and the True Religion, and to cleanse this land of Popish idolatry. It would be a grievous thing if grace were withheld from him who comes after."

For a moment or two Benedict pondered him in silence, his dark face inscrutable. He could see fanaticism in Warner's eyes, and of all human emotions, that filled him with the deepest disgust. He had seen it so often. In the eyes of Catholic priests, of Puritan preachers, of the Holy Men of Islam; and wherever it ruled, with it, like attendant demons, lurked suffering, terror and despair.

"I am no more a lover of Papists, Colonel, than you are," he replied at length, in a tone which betrayed as little emotion as his face, "though perhaps I may claim a more intimate acquaintance with them. For nearly two years I was a prisoner of the Spaniards, and much of that time I spent chained to the rowing-bench of a galley."

Warner looked taken aback. "Then I ask your pardon, sir. You have indeed suffered in the cause."

"That was but one of my nephew's many adventures," Sir Nicholas put in. He felt that the conversation was drifting into dangerous channels, and should be steered elsewhere before the question of Benedict's deliverance from the galleys was raised. "He has travelled the world over, and seen lands and peoples which to us are little more than legends."

"Or travellers' tales," Martin said scornfully under his breath. Mercy, who was the only one to catch the words, looked indignant reproach, and then turned to Benedict.

"And played so many parts," she said admiringly. "Soldier, sailor, even slave. Cousin, tell us what else."

Benedict smiled at her. At first she had shown considerable awe of him, but he had treated her with a skillful blend of gallantry and indulgence which soon overcame her shyness. Now she was showing unmistakable signs of hero-worship, and this amused him. He thought her a likeable child.

"Oh, many things, little cousin," he said lightly. "I have lived among gypsies, and on two different occasions I have been a strolling player . . ."

A scandalised gasp from Edith interrupted him. He realised that the whole company was regarding him with disapproval, and belatedly remembered the aversion with which the theatre was regarded by everyone with the least leaning towards Puritanism. It could not have caused greater outrage if he had disclosed his career as a pirate captain. Possibly, he though cynically, it would have caused less. Many staunchly Puritan merchants owned ships engaged in both piracy and the slave-trade.

"Are you serious, nephew, or is this an ill-timed jest?" Sir Nicholas asked sternly, and Colonel Warner added with a look of loathing:

"Theatres are an abomination of the Devil, sir, and play-actors the most miserable of sinners. I am astounded—nay, I am profoundly shocked—that you should confess to any knowledge of either."

Benedict looked at him with his most saturnine expression. He knew that he ought to tread warily, but Warner's hyprocisy sickened him.

"I have known men to commit worse sins than play-acting, sir," he said with a sneer, "and seen worse places than theatres. If *you* have not, I felicitate you, but take leave to doubt that you have seen very much of the world."

The Colonel's face whitened with anger, but before he could speak Sir Nicholas hastily intervened to change the subject, and after a moment's struggle with himself Warner allowed himself to be diverted. Benedict was torn between exasperation and amusement. He wondered what they would have said had they known that his second venture, soon after he fled from Algiers, could not even be dignified by the name of acting, since it had consisted of performing feats of strength at country fairs. Would that be considered a greater sin, or a lesser? The question was not likely to find an answer.

One thing about which there could be no question at all was the Warners' hostility towards him; or the reason for it. Martin clearly regarded Mercy as his property and resented her interest in her new-found kinsman, while his father's resentment arose from a similar but more worldly cause. Martin was an only son, and Mercy, until Benedict's inopportune return, had been the sole heiress of Monksfield. No doubt the Colonel had been planning an alliance between the two families, the two estates. His disapproval and hostility, like Edith's, were rooted in self-interest, that most powerful of human motives. Benedict could fully understand that; he was himself inspired by a most profound self-interest.

On Sunday he went with the rest of the family to church, and sat patiently through a three-hour sermon loud with that Old Testament savagery so beloved by the more extreme religious sects. The church, which he remembered as rich with carved wood and stained glass, was bare now, its walls starkly whitewashed, its windows plain, so that the light fell, cold and unflattering, over the soberly dressed congregation and the gaunt face and burning eyes of the preacher who had replaced the kindly parson of Benedict's boyhood. The preacher, who had heard of the Squire's nephew lately returned from wandering in heathen lands, was gratified to observe his attentive presence, and never suspected that behind that dark, impassive countenance the gentleman's thoughts and memories were wandering idly among subjects very far removed from his soul's salvation.

Sir Nicholas, too, was gratified. He had been secretly much troubled by the knowledge that Benedict had once practised the Muslim faith, and he had half feared some turning away from Christian beliefs. Now, seeing his nephew apparently devout, he remembered with relief that he had spoken of using the rituals of Islam with no true conviction. It never occurred to Sir Nicholas that a man so contemptuous of one faith might regard all others with equal indifference.

There was, in fact, a good deal which did not occur to the old gentleman where Benedict was concerned, for the younger man had planned his campaign at Monksfield with the same audacity and foresight which had brought him fortune along the Barbary coast. Within an hour of his return he had perceived how his uncle wished to regard him, and since then he had been playing the part with consummate skill. The repentant rebel, drawn home by a sense of duty to comfort the last years of a lonely old man; the last survivor, miraculously preserved to save the name of Forde from extinction; the one-time wastrel, now eager to learn all he could about the management of the estate and to ease the burden it laid on his uncle's ageing shoulders.

He had come hoping, at best, for the younger son's

portion which had been his father's, but as the days lengthened into weeks he began to feel more and more certain that Sir Nicholas would make him his heir. Of course, there was Mercy to be considered, but a girl must marry and a wife's place was with her husband. There had been Fordes at Monksfield for over two hundred years.

Sir Nicholas would undoubtedly demand that Benedict himself should marry, and he had already determined that when the time came, he would fetch Bronwen from London, for she was the one woman who might make bearable the humdrum domestic existence to which he would have condemned himself. There would certainly be difficulties over his decision to take a dowerless bride, but he felt confident that Bronwen herself would soon be able to win his uncle's approval, while there was no doubt that she would be more than a match for Edith.

It seemed that the tide of fortune was running in his favour, yet there were times when, in spite of the richness of the prize he gambled for, he was appalled by the prospect of spending the rest of his life as a country squire. He was a practical man, and if Monksfield were offered to him, he would take it, but he could not delude himself into believing that it would prove an unmixed blessing. He would remain an adventurer at heart, with his gaze for ever fixed on horizons far beyond the small world of village life, but he told himself that when the inevitable restlessness seized upon him, Bronwen would be his salvation.

He was increasingly impatient to return to her. He had forgotten the friction between them in London, the bitterness of their parting quarrel, even the belief that she looked down on him because of his lawless past. All these things were less important to him now than his need of her.

. . . . .

October had drawn to its close. It had been a beautiful month of crisp, bright days and frosty nights, but through it the voice of winter had spoken ever more loudly. Now, with the coming of November, the weather changed, and winter seemed no longer to be merely heralded, but to have arrived. Monksfield seemed to draw in upon itself; to settle, like the countryside around it, into sleep.

Benedict's impatience grew. Sir Nicholas treated him like a son, discussing with him many matters concerning the estate and asking his opinion on them, but no mention had been made of the future. He had not even inquired whether Benedict had any plans of his own, or what these might be, while Edith, her hostility unabated, had even begun to throw out sly hints that, happy though his visit had made his uncle, the time had come to end it.

Benedict found that her watchful malice, and the frequent, resentful presence of Martin Warner—for Edith constantly encouraged the boy to visit them—were beginning to irritate him, while the thought of the inevitable isolation which winter must bring to so remote a district as Monksfield grew less and less enticing. It had been bad enough in the old days, and then there had been a large family, both at Monksfield itself

133

and his own home, and the chill hand of righteousness had lain less heavily upon the neighbourhood. He would endure all this, and more, if there were sure profit at the end of it, but if he did not stand to gain anything he would rather be elsewhere, seeking to fill his purse by other methods which, though more hazardous, were more congenial to a man of his temperament.

Underlying his growing restlessness was the thought of Bronwen, and now he bitterly regretted his hasty decision to part from her. He had been a fool to leave her in London, where, during his absence, she might well find another protector or even a husband. She was not destitute now, or a fugitive fleeing from a danger so terible that it could force her into the arms of the first man she encountered who had the will and the ability to save her from it. She was beautiful enough and clever enough to find someone else, but the thought that she might do so was intolerable. She was his, and he would never let her go.

Uncertainty of one kind and another drove him eventually to a gambler's throw, staking all on the chance of provoking his uncle to definite action. He came in from a long, solitary ride which had failed in its object of assuaging some of the impatience and restlessness which was consuming him, and found the old man sitting alone by the fire in the hall. A bitter wind was driving sheets of rain before it, so that as Benedict swung the cloak from his shoulders for the servant to take, a shower of drops shook down from it to spatter the scrubbed flagstones. He took off his hat with its sodden plume, handed that to the serving-man also, and walked across to spread his hands to the warmth of the great logs blazing on the hearth.

Sir Nicholas, who had been staring into the fire, and stroking the hound which sat with its head resting on his knee, looked quizzically up at him.

"You choose unkindly weather, nephew, in which to ride abroad."

Benedict laughed, "Inactivity irks me, sir. I think it is time for me to begone, before winter closes in upon us completely."

"To begone?" There was no mistaking the dismay in his uncle's voice. "Whither, in pity's name?"

"Back to London first, sir, and then, who knows? Somewhere where there is fighting to be done, by sea or by land. A man must have some purpose in his life."

He was watching Sir Nicholas narrowly without appearing to, and he saw the troubled frown lingering in his face. The old man asked:

"Are you determined to take up arms again?"

Benedict shrugged. "It is the trade I know best."

"Yet you might learn another." Sir Nicholas was silent for a space, idly drawing the dog's ear through his fingers, then, as though coming to a decision, thrust the beast gently aside and stood up, adding abruptly: "Come to the east parlour. We may be private there."

In silence, but with his hopes rising, Benedict obeyed. The oak-panelled parlour was a cosier, more intimate place than the galleried hall, where conversation could be heard by any passing member of the household, and he thought it a good omen that Sir Nicholas wanted to speak privily with him. He waited until the old gentleman had taken a chair on one side of the fireplace, and then sat down opposite him. Mercy's spaniel puppy, which had been sleeping by the hearth until they came in, scrabbled its paws against his booted foot, and he picked the little creature up and set it on his knee. It squirmed and wriggled ecstatically as he fondled it, and worried at his fingers with small, sharp teeth.

"I will be plain with you, nephew," Sir Nicholas began. "You told me when you came home that you had felt it your duty to do so. Why then do you now speak of leaving again?"

"I felt it my duty, sir, to inform you that I still lived, and to discover whether you had any need of me. It was never my intention to live here upon your bounty."

"And have I no need of you?"

Benedict's wide shoulders lifted. "Sir, you are hale and well, and the estate prospers. There is naught for me to do here."

"I may be hale and well," Sir Nicholas retorted tartly, "but I am seventy years of age, and how long do you suppose the estate will continue to prosper when I am no longer here to husband it? I have watched you these past weeks, Benedict. I have set before you such problems as arose, and taken heed of your judgment upon them. It has been sound. You were not reared to the business of governing an estate, as my own sons were, but you have the habit of command and you know how to deal with your fellow men. Therefore I say to you, bide here, learn of me, and when I die, Monksfield shall be yours."

Benedict had been looking at him while he spoke,

136

but now his gaze dropped quickly to the puppy on his knee, for he did not want his uncle to see the elation which he knew had come leaping into his eyes. So he had been right to force the issue. The prize was as good as his.

"Sir, what can I say? Such generosity is more than I deserve—and there is another with a closer claim to Monksfield than my own."

Sir Nicholas made an impatient movement. "The estate had always descended through the male line, and you and I are the last men to bear the name of Forde. Forde of Monksfield! It has been so these two centuries and more."

"True, sir, but Richard was your son, and Mercy is Richard's only child."

"And a green girl, who cannot be left sole mistress of an estate," Sir Nicholas replied testily. "Still, such scruples do you credit, so to set your mind at ease let me tell you that I have already thought on this. Mercy will not be deprived of her inheritance. You shall marry her."

Benedict's strong hands were still suddenly on the puppy's silky fur; his dark gaze leapt to meet his uncle's. "Marry Mercy?" he repeated blankly. "God's pity, sir, I am of an age with her father!"

"What matter for that? A young bride is no bad thing, and your kinship is not so close as to preclude marriage between you. Yes, this will amend all. My great-grandchildren will inherit what is mine, yet there will still be Fordes at Monksfield."

Benedict frowned. "You know something of what

137

my past life has been, yet you offer me this child as my bride?"

"Your past life does not concern me, boy. Treat Mercy well, and it need not concern her, either. I look to the future."

"And the girl herself?"

"She will do as I bid her, but she likes you well. I have already marked that."

"Her mother does not," Benedict said grimly.

"Her mother counts for nothing in this. She hoped to see Mercy married to young Martin Warner, and, truth to tell, if you had not returned I would have agreed to the match." He paused, shrewdly studying Benedict's impassive face. "Well, nephew, what do you say? You are a grown man and I cannot compel you. I tell you what I desire, but the decision must be yours."

Benedict set the puppy down, got up from his chair and walked across to the window, where he stood looking out even though nothing could be seen for the rain which was beating and streaming against the glass. His dark face wore its most forbidding expression, the lines upon it seeming more deeply graven than before. "I cannot compel you," his uncle had said, yet he was doing so very effectively, for, without saying it in so many words, he had made it clear that Mercy and Monksfield were indivisible. Benedict would have to take both, or neither.

And Bronwen? For an instant the memory of her imposed itself upon the steaming panes as vividly as though she stood before him. Bronwen, with her slender white beauty, her hair like a raven's wing, and green eyes mysteriously slanted. Bronwen, the enchantress, the elf-queen. Longing for her ran through him like flame, and the thought of Mercy, plump, pretty child though she was, seemed utterly repellent. Then, with a ruthless effort of will, he banished the tormenting vision. A man of birth did not marry for beauty, or even for shared passion; he married for solid, practical reasons, such as Monksfield's broad acres and comfortable revenues.

He swung round again to face the room; from his chair by the fire Sir Nicholas was expectantly regarding him.

"So be it, uncle," Benedict said quietly, and his deep voice was firm, with no least tremor of hesitation or doubt. "I will do as you desire, and trust I may prove worthy of your faith in me."

*   *   *   *   *   *

"No!" Edith said vehemently. "No, no, no!" With each repetition of the word her voice rose, until she was almost screaming. "You cannot do this—this monstrous thing!"

"Be silent, woman!" Sir Nicholas commanded explosively. "Be silent, or take yourself hence! Do you forget to whom you speak?"

He was very angry, his face darkly flushed, his neat white beard seeming to bristle with the intensity of his rage, so that even Edith's near-hysteria was subdued. She sank down again into the chair from which she had just risen, her thin hands clutching at its arms as she tried to control her horror and dismay. In the corner, Mercy still sat at her spinning-wheel, stunned into silence by her grandfather's announcement and the reaction it had provoked in her mother.

They were in the west parlour, which at Monksfield had for many years been regarded as primarily the women's domain, just as the east parlour belonged to the men.

Through the window could be seen the trees tossing bare branches in the wind and rain driving across the garden, but within the room was bright firelight and, until Sir Nicholas came in, a comfortable accustomed peace. It was strange, Mercy thought confusedly, how suddenly one's whole life could change. She had been spinning, her thoughts wandering idly as she listened to the steady sound of the wheel, while Mother sat sewing in her big chair by the fire. Everything had been ordinary, pleasant and humdrum, and then Grandfather had come, with the bald announcement that Mercy was to marry Cousin Benedict, and Mother had let her sewing fall to the ground as she sprang up to utter that impassioned protest.

Mercy herself was still trying to take in a prospect so totally unexpected that as yet she could not really believe it. She had known, of course, that Grandfather would choose a husband for her, but she had supposed that this would be Martin Warner, and the thought had inspired neither excitement nor dismay. To marry Cousin Benedict, whom she had unconsciously set on a level with her grandfather and Colonel Warner, was a very different matter. She sat silent, scarcely hearing the dispute between Edith and Sir Nicholas, her mind cautiously exploring the startling picture of the future set so suddenly before her.

Edith was doing her best to control her feelings, and to marshal reasoned arguments which might influence Sir Nicholas where horrified protests would only enrage him still more. Gripping her hands tightly together to hide their trembling, and taking a deep breath to steady her voice, she said more calmly:

"I ask your pardon, sir, for a violence of language which sprang solely from a mother's fears, and not from any disrespect towards you."

"Fears?" he repeated irritably. "What fears, pray, should you have simply because I say Mercy is to be married? Did you expect her to live and die a maid?"

"No, never that! I want her to marry, but not such a man as your nephew." She encountered another angry glance and added hastily: "Pray consider, sir. He is older than I, her mother."

He brushed this aside. "Better a man, with a man's judgment and experience, then a hot-headed boy like young Martin. That is what you hoped for, is it not? A match between him and Mercy?"

"I will not deny,' she said carefully, "that I would regard such a marriage with a more hopeful heart than the one you propose for her." She looked imploringly at him. "And it would be a good match, Sir Nicholas. It would unite the two estates, and Martin's faults are only the faults of youth."

"Oh, I have nothing against the boy," Sir Nicholas said impatiently, "and had Benedict not come home, he would have done well enough. But Benedict is my brother's son, the last of our line, and it is right and proper that Monksfield should go to him. Yet I would not have Mercy deprived. So they shall marry, and by

141

the Lord's grace their issue may hold Monksfield for as long as their forebears have done."

Edith cast a quick glance at her daughter, but Mercy did not seem to be listening. She still sat with one foot resting on the treadle of the spinning-wheel, her hands, with the yarn yet in them, lying motionless in her lap, and her blue eyes gazing straight before her with a withdrawn expression in them. Edith could not tell what she was thinking. She leaned forward in her chair, once more gripping the arms of it, and said in a lower tone, but no less urgently:

"Sir Nicholas, I know you have much affection for Mercy. How then can you give her in marriage to a man nearly twenty years older than she, and one who has led so wild and godless a life?"

"Godless?" Sir Nicholas took her up sharply, more sharply than he would have done had his own doubts been wholly laid to rest. "What mean you by that? Has he ever absented himself from family prayers since he has been here, or failed to attend church?"

"He could not do otherwise, if he wishes to stand well with you," Edith retorted shrewdly, "but I am not speaking of the present. What of the years he was away? By his own admission he has travelled in heathen lands. He has been a play-actor. And a seafarer. I grew up in a seaport town, and I know that mariners are not commonly remarkable for godliness."

Sir Nicholas scowled at her. He had never liked Edith even though her marriage to Richard had been of his contriving. She was the only child of a rich merchant of Ipswich, a man who combined avarice with religious fervour of a peculiarly joyless kind, and had reared his daughter in the traditions of both. She had brought Richard a large dowry, Sir Nicholas reflected grimly now, and very little else. No warmth or affection, and, the truly unforgivable thing, no heir. She had borne three children after Mercy, all boys, but not one of them had lived more than a few hours. And the wife chosen for Richard's elder brother had proved wholly barren . . . Sir Nicholas found his thoughts wandering, and jerked them sharply back to the matter in hand.

"I will hear no more of this," he said sternly. "I know that you dislike Benedict, and I thought the reason for that was a pardonable fear that your daughter might be made the poorer by his coming, but you know now that she will not. So hold your peace, and do not try to turn her against him, for that would be to do her a great disservice." He turned from her, and spoke in a kindlier tone: "Mercy, my child, you understand, do you not, the provision I have made for you?"

"Yes, Grandfather." Mercy turned grave blue eyes towards him. "I am to marry my kinsman, and live at Monksfield always."

"And you will obey me without question, as it is your duty to do?"

She nodded solemnly. "Yes, sir, I will. I am glad that I shall not have to leave Monksfield, and—and I like Cousin Benedict."

"Hark to her!" Edith exclaimed bitterly. "Like him, indeed! What can she, poor innocent, know of such a man as that? But you will learn, daughter! In pain and sorrow, you will learn."

"Madam, have done!" Sir Nicholas rounded upon her, this time with such fury that she recoiled, huddling

143

down in her chair as though fearing physical violence. "I shall not warn you again. One word more, and you go back to your father's house in Ipswich until Benedict and Mercy are wed. I will not brook your defiance! I have made the best provision I can, both for her and for Monksfield, since I have no grandson to succeed me."

Edith gave a piteous cry and buried her face in her hands, and Sir Nicholas looked down at her with satisfaction, knowing that he had silenced her at last. He was not a cruel man, and ordinarily would never have referred so brutally to her dead sons, but he had made up his mind to this marriage and was not going to have it put in jeopardy. He gave a final turn to the screw.

"One word more! It would be prudent for you to moderate your attitude towards my nephew. Remember, one day he will be master here." He turned to his grand-daughter. "Come, my child. He is waiting for us."

Mercy got up, but then hesitated, looking at her mother's hunched figure and even taking a tentative step towards her, but Sir Nicholas was holding out his hand in a commanding way, and when Edith did not look up, the girl went past her and let him lead her from the room.

In the hall, Benedict was standing by the fire, staring down into it, and Mercy studied him as her grandfather led her forward, seeing him now not merely as a kinsman but as her future husband. To be sure, he was quite old and not at all handsome—almost ugly, in fact—and she was still just the least bit afraid of him, but how tall he was, and splendid in his rich, dark

144

clothes, with that air about him which made him seem so different from any other man, young or old, that she had ever seen. Not one of her friends would have such a husband, she thought with naive satisfaction.

He turned as they came towards him. Sir Nicholas, his good-humour restored as soon as he was out of his daughter-in-law's presence, said jovially:

"I have told Mercy of my wishes. Come, nephew, give me your hand."

Silently Benedict extended his right hand. Sir Nicholas put Mercy's into it, and for a moment clasped them both between his own. He was clearly much moved.

"This is a day I never thought to see," he said unsteadily. "A glad day, indeed! The Lord has been merciful to me at this, the latter end of my life."

Benedict said nothing. He looked down at their joined hands, and thought cynically how easy it had been to attain his goal. Of all those at Monksfield, only Edith had suspected something of his true worth, his real purpose; and she was now utterly defeated.

Mercy, stealing a shy glance at his face, read something there which somehow intensified the small, illogical stab of fear she had felt as his lean, strong fingers closed upon her own. A fear born of things her mother had said of him; sly, dark hints which Mercy had only half understood, but which now returned confusedly to her mind so that she felt a momentary sense of being trapped, helpless in the power of some dark and unknown force.

He felt her hand tremble suddenly in his, and, glancing swiftly at her face, saw alarm clearly written there.

An alarm which must be soothed, for it would not do for her to fear him.

"I am aware, sir, how precious is the charge you now place upon me," he said, and though the words were addressed to Sir Nicholas, it was to Mercy that he spoke, his voice gentle, warm, infinitely reassuring. "Be sure that I shall guard her well."

He saw alarm fade from her eyes, and then colour steal into her cheeks as her gaze dropped shyly away from his. He stooped and kissed her gently on the lips—and thought of Bronwen.

•　　　•　　　•　　　•　　　•

Benedict was riding back to Monksfield from Bury St. Edmunds. Riding slowly, because wind and rain had been followed during that day by a sudden calm, and the spreading of a thick, white mist across the countryside, so that it would be all too easy to mistake an unfamilar road. It was cold, too, and the daylight was fading. He found it pleasant to think of Monksfield, where fires would be blazing cheerfully in panelled rooms, and good food and good wine awaited him. Pleasant to think of the inheritance which would one day be his.

His, at the price of freedom. He brushed the thought impatiently aside. He had had twenty years of freedom, and what was there to show for it? He had known the extremes of wealth and poverty; he had suffered and he had sinned; he had returned finally, with purse nearly empty and mind wholly devoid of faith or conscience, to the place whence he had set out; and there, and

146

there only, had he found a way to lasting profit. To be sure, it was the way of trickery and deceit, and of pretending religious convictions for which he felt only contempt, but what was that to a man without honour, a man who feared neither God nor Devil because he had no hope of heaven or dread of hell?

Two days had passed since he agreed to marry Mercy, and already Sir Nicholas was pressing ahead with arrangements for their wedding. Yesterday he had summoned his lawyer and set him to drawing up a new Will and drafting marriage settlements, and when the man had gone, promising to prepare the documents with all possible despatch, Sir Nicholas had clapped Benedict on the shoulder.

"I fear, lad, that to a lawyer, haste is what other men call sloth, but no matter for that. You shall be wed before Christmastide."

Edith, who was present, looked dismayed, and protested that the necessary preparations could not be so quickly completed. Sir Nicholas gave a snort of scornful laughter.

"Nonsense, nonsense! You have been busy about Mercy's dower-chest these five years past, and for the rest, what preparations are needful? It is no longer the custom to celebrate a wedding with feasting and merry-making. More is the pity!"

"For shame, Sir Nicholas!" Edith spoke sharply, for she was never afraid to take issue with him when she considered him to be backsliding in matters of religion. "Such heathenish rites and lewd customs are an offence in the eyes of the Lord."

"There was nothing amiss with the old ways," he

replied obstinately. "They were a trifle boisterous, perhaps, but none the worse for that. A wedding should be a time of rejoicing." A reminiscent look came into his eyes. "I well remember my own. That was fifty years ago and more, in the old Queen's time, when Englishmen still knew how to make merry."

Edith rose to her feet with an air of cold rebuke. "Never did I think to hear such words again beneath this roof! It is plain to see, Sir Nicholas, whence comes this influence of ungodliness. I will stay to hear no more."

She cast a venomous glance at Benedict and went out. Sir Nicholas looked at his nephew.

"She seeks to create difficulties where none exist," he remarked, "but to no avail. I have said you and Mercy shall be wed by Christmastide, and wed you shall be."

Benedict was frowning. "Before then, sir, I must return briefly to London, to fetch my servant and the rest of my gear. The sooner the better, before winter sets in."

"Must you go? Can you not trust your servant to come to you, if you send him word?"

"I could, but if I am to dwell here henceforth, there are some matters in London which must be settled, and only I can deal with them. It will take only a few days, but I must go myself."

He had spoken with finality, and Sir Nicholas, though looking at him very hard, offered no further argument. Benedict thought he probably suspected that his nephew's business in London in some way concerned a woman, and approved of his supposed intention to free himself of all such entanglements before his marriage. It was just as well, Benedict reflected cynically, that the old man could not guess the real purpose of his journey.

He had no intention of giving up Bronwen, even though he had relinquished the idea of making her his wife. If he could not have Monksfield without marrying Mercy, then he would marry her, but Bronwen was vital to him in a way no other woman could ever be. For Monksfield he would surrender his freedom; surrender the wide world which called to him still with the siren voice of adventure; he would not, could not surrender the beauty and the mystery which was Bronwen. Quarrel they might, despise him she might, but the thought of life without her was intolerable.

The practical details of establishing her in Suffolk were easy enough to plan. Before he could fetch her from London, a home must be found for her. A small, comfortable house with one or two discreet servants, far enough from Monksfield for her presence to remain unsuspected by his family, yet near enough to be within easy reach. That had been the purpose of to-day's visit to Bury St. Edmunds.

He had chosen that town because the Fordes had no connections there, all their interests lying rather towards the coast. By diligent searching and the free spending of his remaining gold he had succeeded in finding what he sought, and by late afternoon the necessary arrangements had been made. He had used an assumed name, and given a convincing account of the reasons which were leading him to establish his household in Bury, and such was his assurance, his air

149

of being accustomed to command, that no one had ventured to question the truth of it. So now he rode homewards, content in the knowledge that on the morrow he could set out for London, and totally untroubled by any pangs of conscience, or remorse for the deception he was practising upon his uncle and his intended bride. Or, for that matter, for the abysmal selfishness of his attitude towards Bronwen herself.

It was dark by the time he reached Monksfield, and in the courtyard, the mist swirled so thickly that the torches which burned in iron sconces on either side of the porch showed faint and dull until he stood directly beneath them. At the sound of his arrival, a groom came running to take charge of his horse, and Benedict strode under the porch and into the lighted hall, savouring already a sense of mastery.

When he entered, Sir Nicholas was just crossing the hall, but he paused and waited for the younger man to join him.

"You come late, Benedict," he greeted him. "I had begun to fear that you had mistaken the road in this mist. It is easily done, especially when one has been so long away."

"I did not lose my way, sir, but I had to go warily for fear of doing so. It is an ill night to be abroad."

"As others besides you have found," Sir Nicholas agreed with a smile. "Already we give shelter to two benighted travelers, a lady and her servant on their way to Ipswich to take ship for Holland. Their guide deserted them, and they wandered, totally lost, until by a fortunate chance they stumbled upon this house.

Come now, and let me present you to the lady. She is with Edith and Mercy in the west parlour."

"A more fortunate chance than she deserved, if she was fool enough to persist in her journey instead of seeking shelter," Benedict said with a touch of impatience as they went on across the hall. "The mist has been thickening since noon."

Sir Nicholas nodded his agreement on the folly of women, and threw open the parlour door. Edith was sitting by the fire, and Mercy standing nearby with their guest, who had her back to the door. Benedict, following his uncle into the room, was stopped dead in his tracks by the sight of a slender figure in a deep purple riding-habit, of a proudly poised head crowned with coils of gleaming, blue-black hair which seemed almost too heavy for the slim, white column of her neck. He stood and stared, his mind reeling with shock. It could not be. It was impossible, unthinkable, a chance likeness which would be dispelled the moment he saw her face. Then she turned, and across the room he found himself meeting the faintly challenging gaze of Bronwen's wide, green, slanted eyes.

Part Six

Benedict was pacing his bedchamber, prowling to and fro like some restless, caged animal, and all the while questions beat mercilessly, maddeningly in his mind. Why had she come? What did she intend? How dare she arrive, without warning, at his uncle's house, calling herself Mrs Aldon and telling a trumped-up tale of a husband awaiting her in Ipswich; of a treacherous guide, a lost road, and a chance arrival at Monksfield's hospitable door.

Chance! He gave a snort of angry, derisive laughter. A chance as carefully planned as his own campaign to become his uncle's heir. A campaign which now, on the very point of success, was put in peril by Bronwen's coming, by the likelihood of her learning of his forthcoming marriage. If he were able to break the news to her himself, in his own way at his own time, he was confident that he could persuade her to accept the situation, but if she discovered it in any other way, would he ever be able to convince her that he had not meant to abandon her? If he could not, it would need but one word from her to lay his whole future in ruins.

Yet would she speak that word? In the hours which had passed since he walked into the west parlour and found her there, she had said nothing, done nothing to betray that she knew him. He had almost betrayed himself in that first, appalled moment; only his long-established habit of self-command had enabled him to dissemble his shock, as it had helped him to get through the subsequent interminable evening without giving himself away, but beneath the imperturbable surface, anger and uncertainty had been steadily growing. Why? When would the blow fall? Would it fall at all?

Bronwen had been the perfect guest, smiling, gracious and charming. He had seen her in many guises, but now he was seeing her for the first time in that to which she had been reared, a lady of quality whose presence would have graced a palace.

He was not the only one to remark this. There had been a bad moment after supper when Mercy, drawing him aside, had whispered:

"Cousin, I think Mrs Aldon cannot be what she pretends. Do *you* believe that she is a merchant's wife?"

He evaded the question, answering it with another. "What do you believe her to be?"

"Some great lady, a noblewoman, going to join her husband in exile. Why else would she be travelling with but one servant, and that a man? Even a merchant's wife would have a maid."

Benedict frowned. "Better keep such fancies to yourself, my girl. If it were true, *we* would want no part in it, and in any event it is discourteous to doubt the word of a guest."

Mercy, abashed by the rebuke, had said no more, but Benedict reflected that her thought showed more perception than he would have given her credit for. A great lady. Tonight Bronwen certainly had the look of it, and since her origins were shrouded in mystery, who could say that she was not? Sir Nicholas was plainly enchanted, Mercy fascinated, and even Edith warmed to a comparatively amiable mood. Once Benedict found Bronwen looking at him with a trace of mockery in her eyes, as though it amused her to find herself so readily accepted by his family.

All of which did nothing to reassure him. He might, he thought, learn something from Joseph, but Joseph was nowhere to be seen, and Benedict knew that he could not summon the supposed Mrs Aldon's servant, or go in search of him, without arousing the curiosity he was so anxious to avoid.

So the evening had dragged to its end, and now the household had retired and his questions were still unanswered. Why? What was she doing here? After the manner of their parting in London, did she mean him good or ill? How long would it be before she found out that he was promised to Mercy? If she had wanted to punish him, she was succeeding only too well; anger and uncertainty had him upon the rack.

And not anger and uncertainty alone. While Bron-

154

wen was in London and he at Monksfield it had been hard enough to put the thought of her to the back of his mind; now she was here, under the same roof, and the knowledge was like a fever in his blood, a consuming flame which no effort of will could subdue. All the evening, in spite of his anxiety, he had seen no one but her, and even when he forced himself to look elsewhere her voice, her laughter, her mere presence continued to tantalise him. His uncle, Edith, Mercy, the servants had all been but shadows on the edge of his consciousness, and Bronwen the only reality.

He paused at last in his restless pacing and stood leaning his hands against the top of the fireplace, staring down at the smouldering logs. His fingers clenched on the dark, carved wood until the knuckles shone like polished stone.

"Damn you, Bronwen!" he muttered. "And damn whatever demon of mischief brought you here! Am I to risk everything I have gained, for the sake of your white body and green, witch's eyes?"

For a time he stood there, fighting a battle which he had known all along he could not win, but in the end he straightened his big shoulders, and his lips twisted in mockery of his own weakness as he turned to extinguish the candles. He waited a few moments to accustom his eyes to the darkness, and then moved softly to the door and opened it, and went, silent as a prowling cat, through the shadows of the sleeping house.

·   ·   ·   ·   ·

The bedchamber allotted to Bronwen was in an adjacent corridor. No gleam of light showed beneath its door, and when he lifted the latch and thrust the door gently open, he found the room in darkness save for a dying fire. As he paused on the threshold he was aware of a slight movement on the far side of the room, where the curtains had been thrown back from the window to leave a patch of greyness on the surrounding gloom. He closed the door softly and went slowly towards it.

Outside, the mist still swirled and drifted against the glass, but it was thinner now, and luminous from the light of an unseen full moon which thrust silvery fingers through it with an effect indescribably ghostly and weird. That faint, reflected radiance showed him Bronwen standing beside the window. A robe of pale, shimmering satin clothed her from throat to foot, and her loosened hair flowed down her back, darker than darkness itself. As he came towards her she said in a low voice:

"I have been waiting for you."

He halted a couple of yards from her. "Were you so certain I would come?"

"I was certain." He could not see her face, save as a pale blur, but he could tell from her voice that she was smiling, with faint mockery in eyes and lips. "If only to discover why I have come here."

"Why did you come?"

"To bring you warning." She was not smiling now; her voice had changed, become urgent. "Benedict, some danger threatens you."

"*Some* danger?" he repeated, frowning. "How, and from whom?"

"I do not know," she replied in a troubled voice. "I

156

would to God I did, for then there might be some means of evading it. Yet danger there is, and that to your very life." She paused, but when he made no reply, added vehemently, "Benedict, you know that at times I have power to foresee the future."

"I know that you believe you have."

"You may believe it, too, for the power is in me. I swear it! I cannot escape it, and there is no escape from the things it shows me. Four days ago it came upon me. I saw you, bound hand and foot, and confronting you was a man I had never seen before, although in some strange way his face seemed familiar to me. And I knew, as surely as though the words had been spoken in my ear, that he was your enemy and held over you the power of life and death."

In spite of himself, in spite of all the promptings of reason, misgiving touched him with a small, cold finger. Speaking with such utter conviction, such quiet certainty, she convinced him whether he would or no. When she had first told him of her strange, unwanted gift he had accepted her word that she possessed, or was possessed by, some inexplicable power; how then could he doubt it now, simply because her vision had concerned himself? Of one thing at least he was completely certain. Bronwen herself believed it.

"If you fear for my safety," he said slowly, "why did you not send Joseph to warn me? You must have known that to arrive here unannounced would create difficulties."

"How could I tell Joseph you are in danger without disclosing how I came by my knowledge? That I dared not do. I might have given him a letter to carry to you,

157

but could any letter convince you of the urgency of my warning?" She paused, and when she spoke again there was bitterness in her voice. "Ah, why do I pretend? I came because I must. Because if you are in danger I wanted to be here to faee it with you."

"Bronwen!"' He took a step towards her, but she drew back, one arm outstretched to hold him off.

"'Benedict, listen to me! The picture is not clear, but one thing more I do know. It is here in this house that danger will face you. I felt it the instant I crossed the threshold."

"I have no enemy in this house—or rather, no man here is my enemy. Edith Forde bears me no goodwill, it's true."

"I do not think it is Mrs Forde who threatens you, or any at her bidding. Yet the danger is very near." With a sudden, desperate gesture she pressed her hands to her eyes. "Oh, why can I not see more clearly? Always it is thus! One glimpse, as though for an instant a curtain had been plucked aside, and then no more, no matter how hard I strive."

"This man, this enemy you say I have," Benedict said abruptly. "What like is he?"

Bronwen lowered her hands, spread them out in a helpless gesture. "Benedict, I do not know! While the vision lasted I saw him clearly, but now I can recall only that I did see him, not what he was like, though of one thing I am certain. If I met with him, I would know his face again."

There was a tautness in her voice which warned him of self-control strained to breaking point. He said with deliberate lightness:

"Scant comfort in that, since for all we know you may never meet with him. Sweetheart, I think you are distressing yourself needlessly. What if your vision does prove true, and I find myself this man's prisoner? I have been a prisoner before, and taken no lasting hurt."

"If only I could believe that," she said in a low voice, "but your danger is real and very great. I have known it all along, and tonight, in this house, I feel it as never before." She moved suddenly, came to him, reached up to grip him by the shoulders. "Benedict, leave this place! It is here your peril lies. I know it! I feel it!"

His arms went round her, holding her hard against him; and he buried his face against the silky blackness of her hair.

"You know not what you ask," he muttered. "My uncle is to make me his heir."

"I know," she whispered. "His heir—on condition that you marry his grand-daughter."

He was startled and dismayed; his hold on her slackened. "Who told you so?"

"Mercy herself. She seemed eager to talk of her approaching bridal."

He was aware of a surge of anger against Mercy which he knew was unjustified. Of course she had been eager to talk, to confide in a supposedly married woman only a few years older than herself, who might be more sympathetic than her own mother. No, if Bronwen had been hurt, it was not Mercy who was to blame.

"Bronwen," he said gently, "I never meant you to

159

learn of it in that fashion. I was coming to London. I intended to set out in the morning."

Drawing her close again, he began to tell her of the plans he had made, speaking gently, tenderly, putting into his voice all the persuasion he could command. She stood quiet in his arms, her head resting against his chest, while he stroked her hair and described to her the house he had found, the little house with its walled garden which was to be her home. The magic of his beautiful voice flowed over her, pleading, reassuring, creating for her a picture so enticing that when at length he paused, she sighed and stirred as though waking from a pleasant dream. "If it could be," she murmured. "Oh, Benedict, if it could only be!"

"It can be, sweetheart, and it will," he insisted. "In the morning, when it is time for you to set out, I will offer to escort you to Ipswich. Then, once away from here, we can turn instead towards Bury."

"No!" She seemed to rouse herself with an effort, to shake off the spell he had cast over her. "Benedict, you cannot, you must not ignore my warning! Is any inheritance worth the imperilling of your life?"

"Is an inheritance such as Monksfield to be cast away because of a mere foreboding of danger?" he countered. "Besides, where would we find the means to travel hence? I spent the last of my money to secure the house in Bury."

"There is the gold you took from Thomas Barnes. I brought it with me. Joseph has charge of it."

"Stolen gold!" he retorted with a flash of the old bitterness. "Have you indeed subdued your conscience to that extent?"

160

"I would turn thief myself if need be, to provide the means to take you out of danger," she said with passionate earnestness. "That accursed gold had stood between us too long. Let us at last turn it to good account."

"I shall never cease to marvel at the complexity of a woman's mind," he said wryly. "The gold is yours—Sir Edwin Aldon's gold, for you, his foster-child—but you despised it, and me with it. Yet now you would use it. A thief's plunder to save a thief's life."

"I would use any means to save you," she replied with a catch in her voice. "I would give my own life, if need be . . . ! Oh. Benedict, do not scoff at my warning, for the power that showed me your danger does not lie!" She reached up to take his face between her hands; her whispered words came brokenly, blurred with tears. "My love, my love, come away with me! Forget this inheritance which carries with it the shadow of death."

"To what purpose," he said softly, "if there is no escape from what you have foreseen? If it is to be, it will be, no matter where I seek to hide from it."

"I understand," she said tragically. "You believe I am prompted by jealousy. That I seek to lure you away from Monksfield and from your intended bride." She wrenched herself suddenly from his embrace and backed away. "Fool! Do you not see that if that were my purpose I would need only to tell your uncle the truth?"

"I know it." His voice was still soft, but with the faintest undertone of menace. "Do not threaten me,

161

Bronwen, unless you are prepared to make good your threat."

"Can you be sure that I am not?" Her voice broke again, choked on a sob. "Benedict, do not force me to a betrayal I know you would never forgive. I will use any means, even that, if you drive me to it."

"Will you?" He moved swiftly, caught her in his arms again before she could retreat further. His own voice was unsteady. "Would you indeed betray me?"

He crushed her against him, his lips urgent on her tear-wet cheeks and trembling mouth until her resistance crumbled, and he was aware of her yielding, her quickening response. At that moment the prize he had schemed for seemed unsubstantial as a dream, and here in his arms was the only true reality.

*　　　*　　　*　　　*　　　*

Yet in the chill grey light of a wintry dawn, alone again in his own room, he cursed himself for a fool. The question was still unresolved, the choice still to be made between abandoning the prize now almost within his grasp and taking the risk of Bronwen disclosing the truth to his uncle.

He did not delude himself into thinking her threat an empty one, or that he had dissuaded her from carrying it out. She believed so implicitly in her own prophetic powers that an ordinary, meaningless dream of a kind which came to everyone at some time or another had been invested in her imagination with all the inevitability of a warning of doom, and she would go to any lengths to save him from the fancied danger. Last night, in the delight of having her in his arms again after the weeks of separation, Monksfield and all it stood for had seemed unimportant, but now, with desire fulfilled and her strange beauty no longer bemusing his senses, he could think more clearly, take stock of everything he was being asked to sacrifice.

There was so little time for argument or persuasion. She would be expected to resume her journey that morning, but he knew that she would not go unless he agreed to go with her; and unless he agreed she would divulge the truth to Sir Nicholas. If only he could think of some means of delaying her departure, of gaining a respite in which he might find some way out of the impasse.

The respite was to be granted to him, through no effort of his own. It was a thoroughly unpleasant morning, for not only was the countryside still shrouded in mist, but there had been a heavy frost, so that twigs and branches which yesterday had dripped moisture were now sheathed in ice, and ice, too, coated the puddles and made the thick mire hard and treacherous underfoot. Sir Nicholas, having stepped out to take stock of the weather, said bluntly that it was no day for a lady to be travelling and that Mrs Aldon must remain at Monksfield until conditions improved. Benedict agreed whole-heartedly.

Bronwen, though making a pretence of reluctance, was equally relieved, for she, too, had been wishing for an excuse to delay a decision which would be so bitterly hard to make. A decision which, though it might save Benedict's life, would inevitably part them for ever.

163

She summoned Joseph, ostensibly to inform him of her altered plans, and received him alone in the west parlour while Edith and Mercy were occupied elsewhere. When she told him that they were to remain at Monksfield until the weather improved, he bowed in acknowledgment of her commands, but then asked:

"When we do leave, madam, will my master go with us?"

Bronwen sighed. "Joseph, I do not know. It is my hope, indeed, my prayer that he will, but . . ." She paused, giving him a straight look. "Do you know how matters stand here?"

He bowed again, and spread his hands in a deprecating gesture. "Madam, I have talked with the other servants. I am told that my master is to marry the young lady, and that one day this house will be his." He looked at her, his dark eyes troubled. "Madam, you know and I know that it will not serve. This is not the life for him."

"Why, so I think, and I believe that in his heart he knows it, too, but he cannot bring himself to give up so rich an inheritance." She hesitated, wondering how far she might safely confide in him without giving him cause to fear or distrust her. "Joseph, I followed him from London because I believe that there is danger for him here. I have a foreboding of disaster, so beseech you, be watchful. Much may depend upon you."

"You may trust me, madam. My master and I have come through many dangers together."

She smiled faintly. "I'll warrant you have! Do you know where I may find him now?"

"He left the house, madam, more than a half-hour

since. I heard him tell Sir Nicholas, when the old gentleman wondered that he should go out on such a day, that he could not stay mewed up withindoors."

Bronwen thanked him and sent him away. She guessed that Benedict was avoiding her, that he sought solitude in order to make up his mind what to do, and resigned herself to waiting with such patience as she could command until he chose to return to the house. She could understand his frame of mind. To have Monksfield within one's grasp, and to abandon it for no better reason than a vague prophecy of danger, could be no easy thing to do.

She expected him to return in time to dine, but when she and the other women and Sir Nicholas gathered in the hall just before the dinner-hour there was still no sign of him. As the minutes passed Edith began to complain of his tardiness, and Sir Nicholas said impatiently:

"Very well, we will not stay for him. Mrs Aldon, allow me to lead you to table."

Bronwen rose from her chair, but as she took the old gentleman's proffered hand they were startled by an imperative knocking at the main door. A serving-man hurried to open it, and Sir Nicholas and his companions paused, waiting to see who came. There was a brief delay, and then the servant reappeared, ushering in the visitor.

He entered briskly, a man of medium height and soldierly appearance, for there was a glimpse of leather buff-coat beneath his heavy cloak. He wore a high-crowned hat starkly innocent of any ornament, but he removed this when he saw the women, and Bronwen

165

stood frozen, staring, her eyes dilating with horror. She knew that face, lean and hollow-cheeked in its frame of straight, silver-flecked fair hair, with its long, cleft chin, ruthless mouth and pale, close-set eyes. Saw it now in the flesh as she had seen it five days ago through her strange power of pre-vision. The face of Benedict's enemy.

For a few seconds her sight dimmed and her surroundings reeled crazily about her, so that she was only half aware of Sir Nicholas stepping forward, of his perplexed but courteous words of greeting. She fought the weakness with all the strength of her will, realising the desperate need to keep her wits about her, and then, as the fleeting dizziness passed, she became aware that the newcomer had not answered Sir Nicholas. He was staring past him as though Forde did not exist, and that his gaze was fixed on her. He had the coldest eyes she had ever seen.

"So!" he said at length, and the icy satisfaction in his level voice made her shiver as though a chill hand had been laid upon her flesh. "I have run you to earth at last, you hell-born slut!" For a moment longer the cold gaze devoured her, and then he turned to Sir Nicholas, saying abruptly: "Your pardon, sir, and yours, ladies. I forget my manners. Permit me to present myself. My name is Aldon. Colonel Giles Aldon."

Bronwen gasped, and then pressed her hand to her lips, fighting a wild, hysterical desire to laugh. The irony of it, that she had been shown this man as Benedict's mortal enemy, with no hint that he was even more an enemy of her own. Giles Aldon. Sir John's

166

younger brother, uncle to the dead Francis. The relentless pursuer, who must have continued the hunt long after they had supposed it abondoned, and had at length brought his quarry to bay.

Sir Nicholas, who had uttered an angry protest at the Colonel's first words, was now utterly nonplussed. He looked in bewilderment from one to the other.

"Aldon?" he repeated. "Colonel *Aldon?* Then you and this lady . . . !"

"She is no kin of mine," the other man broke in coldly. "She has no right to our name, nor ever had. She is the bastard brat of some nameless trollop befriended by my kinsman, and reared in the hall instead of the kennel where she belongs, but that is the least of it. I must warn you, sir, that in giving her shelter you are guilty of harbouring a witch."

Edith uttered a stifled scream, and Mercy, who had been standing close to Bronwen, shrank away, turning to her mother, who flung a protective arm about her. Sir Nicholas had lost a little of his high colour, but said stoutly:

"That, sir, is a grievous charge to bring against any woman, and one of which I shall need a deal more proof than a stranger's unsupported word."

Colonel Aldon bowed slightly. "Such scruples, sir, are only to be expected, but I shall not ask you to accept my word alone. First, my identity. Since I was coming to a part of the country where neither my name nor my credit is known, I took the precaution, before leaving London, of furnishing myself with credentials." He produced a folded paper and handed it to Sir Nich-

167

olas, adding with a touch of irony: "You will not, I think, presume to question the authority of *that* name."

Sir Nicholas, who had taken the document reluctantly enough, unfolded it and looked curiously at the name it bore. His eyes widened.

"Oliver Cromwell," he read aloud, and Edith and Mercy gasped, and peered over his shoulder to stare with awe at the signature of the most powerful man in all England, while Sir Nicholas looked again at Aldon. "That is indeed a name to command respect," he said gravely. "My house is honoured, sir, by the presence of a friend of the Lord General."

He paused inquiringly, but before the Colonel could speak, Bronwen said in a high, strained voice:

"Sir Nicholas, I have never seen this gentleman in my life until now."

"That is true," Aldon agreed calmly, "though I recognise you without difficulty from the descriptions of those who have had the misfortune to know you. One of them is with me now." He raised his voice a little. "Thomas!"

There was the sound of a heavy tread, and the corpulent, powerful figure and arrogant moustache of Thomas Barnes came into view round the screens. He crossed the hall to where they stood, and looked at Bronwen with a curious mingling of hatred and fear.

"You know this young woman, Thomas, I believe?" Aldon said in an expressionless voice.

"Aye, sir. 'Tis Bronwen the witch. She who sent her Devil's imp to murder poor Mr Francis, and laid a curse on your brother, Sir John, and all his family. The witch the Devil snatched from us just as we were going to cast her into the mill-pool."

"He lies," Bronwen said desperately. "I swear before God that I am no witch." She swung round to Sir Nicholas. "Sir, it is I who have suffered at the hands of the Aldons, not they at mine. When my foster-father died, they robbed me and drove me out of my home, and now bring these false charges against me so that they may be rid of me for ever."

"Lies, is it?" Barnes retorted. "Let the people of Twyning Green bear witness to the truth of what I say. The children who heard you threaten Mr Francis the day before you killed him, and all those who saw the Devil's mark upon your body." He turned to Sir Nicholas. "You want proof, your Honour, that she is a black witch? Strip off her fine clothes, and lay bare the mark o' Satan she carries beneath her breast."

He took a step towards her as though to carry out the threat, and Bronwen instinctively recoiled. Sir Nicholas thrust his arm between them.

"Hold, there!" he said angrily. "If such examination prove needful, it shall be carried out at the proper place and time. Meanwhile, this lady is still a guest beneath my roof, and shall not be subjected to insult and humiliation at the bidding of an upstart knave."

The Colonel gestured imperiously to Barnes to draw back, and the big man obeyed, looking sullen. Aldon addressed Sir Nicholas.

"We do not desire, sir, to take the law into our own hands, but would it not abate your doubts if such proof were forthcoming? Perhaps if your women servants

were to search her, in the presence of this lady . . . ?"
He bowed slightly in Edith's direction.

"That is not necessary," Bronwen interrupted, and
though her voice was still taut with tension, it was
quite steady. "I do not deny that I bear a birthmark—
for that is all it is. I have been told that my mother
bore it also."

"You convict yourself, woman!" Aldon told her
grimly. "It is well known that the taint of witch-hood is
often passed from mother to daughter for generations."

"What of the man, Colonel?" Barnes put in sullenly.
"The warlock who came from nowhere to snatch her
from us and carry her off into the forest? A tall man,
your Honour," he added to Sir Nicholas, "clad all in
black and scarlet and riding a great black horse. I tell
you, 'twas a sight to strike terror into the hearts of
honest men."

"I knew it!" Edith, until now silent and awe-
stricken, cried out suddenly with shrill triumph. "I
knew he was evil the first moment I saw him! What of
your fine nephew now, Sir Nicholas? This is the man
whom you would have made your heir, and given my
daughter in marriage!"

"Peace, woman!" Sir Nicholas said hoarsely. His
usually ruddy cheeks were ashen now as he looked
from Barnes to Bronwen's white face. "We cannot
know it was he . . ."

Giles Aldon was watching him, his light eyes slightly
narrowed and holding a calculating expression. After a
moment he said sternly: "You are too hasty, Thomas.
It is yet to be established whether the man is indeed a
warlock, or merely another hapless victim of this
170

woman's hellish powers. We already know, from the fate of my poor nephew, Francis, that she has potent spells at her command to lure men to destruction."

Mercy, who had been listening with frightened bewilderment, said protestingly: "But Cousin Benedict and Mrs Aldon did not meet until yesterday."

"The woman Bronwen," Colonel Aldon said with icy emphasis, "followed Benedict Forde here from London. It was he who saved her from the just anger of her neighbours and carried her off, no one knows whither. What *is* known is that a month later they appeared in London, where they consorted together in lewd and amorous dalliance until he left her to come here. This is a matter of established fact, as any number of witnesses will testify."

"So," Edith exclaimed triumphantly, "at last we have the truth concerning our returned prodigal! A dabbler in the black arts, the lover of a known witch, with the effrontery to bring his hell-hag here. Do you not see, Sir Nicholas, the peril from which, by the Lord's grace, we have been preserved? She is a witch and a murderess! How long do you suppose *you* would have lived, once he was certain of inheriting Monksfield?"

Sir Nicholas, grey-faced, had dropped down into his chair by the fire. He seemed to have shrunk, as though suddenly feeling for the first time the full weight of his years. It was Giles Aldon who answered Edith's denunciation.

"Let us not judge Benedict Forde too hastily, madam," he said. "I do not believe he summoned the witch here, for how could that serve his interests? Is it not more likely that she, learning by her devilish arts that he is to marry your daughter, came here to prevent it? She tried to lure my nephew into marriage, and when he refused her, she killed him. It may be that my coming has saved Mr Forde himself from mortal peril."

In spite of the cold paralysis of terror which was creeping over her, Bronwen was still capable of feeling surprise at Aldon's words. He seemed anxious to exonerate Benedict, heaping the whole blame upon her. No mention had yet been made of the waylaying of Thomas Barnes, or the stolen gold which was even now in this house, in Joseph's care.

Joseph! The name rang in her mind like a trumpet-call, rousing her numbed wits to life. She lifted her head and looked about her. Word of what was happening in the hall must have spread, in the way such things did spread in a large household, for servants were gathering stealthily in doorways and corners, staring and whispering, but though her gaze swept anxiously from one group to another, she could not see Joseph among them. Had he already summed up the situation, and hastened to search for and warn his master? She could only pray that he had, and that Benedict would heed the warning. She longed for him now as never before; for the comfort of his presence; for the ready wit and the strong arm which hitherto had kept her safe, but she knew that she was trapped beyond all hope of salvation. The horror from which she had fled on that evening of fear and storm had been evaded for only a little while; it had bided its time and was now about to engulf her completely; and if Benedict tried to save her he could accomplish nothing but his own destruction.

Giles Aldon was speaking again, recounting in detail the supposed proof of her witch-hood. He told it without heat, in a level, unemotional voice which carried more conviction than any wrathful denunciation, and as Bronwen listened to him her last hope died. In that superstitious age, men like Benedict were rare. The vast majority, of which Sir Nicholas was plainly one, believed implicitly in witchcraft and saw nothing incredible in charges such as those now being made against her. By the time Aldon had done, she knew that everyone in the hall, from Sir Nicholas himself to the humblest servant, was convinced of her guilt. The old man's first words confirmed it. "What is your intention, sir?" he asked when Aldon paused. "Will you take her hence?"

"I will, Sir Nicholas. She must be returned to Essex, to answer for her crimes in the place where they were committed. You will see that General Cromwell's letter gives me authority to take whatever measures I deem needful." He paused, and then added with only the faintest inflection of apology: "I fear I must take your nephew also. It has yet to be established whether he is accomplice or victim, and in either case his evidence will be required. Will you be good enough to summon him?"

"He is not in the house," Sir Nicholas replied dully. "He went out, I do not know where."

"Then we will await his return, and while we wait, the witch must be bestowed in some secure place, and a close watch to be kept to see whether her imps and familiars come to her."

Sir Nicholas beckoned one of the serving-men to him. "You heard what has passed here. Take the witch and imprison her in the moat cellar, and some of you keep watch outside the door."

He did not look at Bronwen as he spoke, but Giles Aldon was watching her with a cold blaze of triumph in his eyes. The memory of that look went with her as the men, Thomas Barnes foremost among them, laid hold upon her and dragged her from the hall and out to the kitchen quarters. Here they paused while one of their number fetched a lantern, and then they went on again, down winding steps to cellars where the stonework was massive and ancient, more ancient by far than the timbered house above. At last the man with the lantern halted and thrust open a door of iron-studded oak, and they flung her headlong into the black hole that gaped beyond. The door crashed shut with a hollow, booming sound which seemed to Bronwen like the very voice of doom, and she was left to utter darkness, bitter cold, and silence broken only by the drip of water somewhere close at hand. To loneliness and terror and the certainty of suffering and death.

·　　　·　　　·　　　·　　　·　　　ⁱ

Benedict, when he left the house, rode only as far as a small hedge-tavern a mile or so away, for in spite of what he had told his uncle he had no particular wish to be out of doors. All he wanted was to be away from

Monksfield, away from Bronwen's disturbing presence and from the beautiful old house which could be his; the inheritance she was asking him to abandon; which she was trying to force him to abandon.

At that hour and in that weather the tavern was empty except for the landlord, who sat by the fire in the big room which served the three-fold purpose of taproom, kitchen and dining-room. He gaped to see the Squire's nephew enter his humble establishment, but recovered sufficiently to bring him the ale he demanded, and to lay fresh logs on the fire. That done, he retreated to the far end of the room, prepared to wait in respectful silence until it pleased the gentleman to notice him again.

He waited a long time. Benedict, wrestling with a problem which seemed insuperable, neglected to call for more ale when his tankard was empty, and the landlord's hopes of profit began to fade. He did not know that Benedict was oblivious of his presence, of his own surroundings, of everything, in fact, but the decision which must somehow be reached. A decision which hung upon one unanswerable question. Would Bronwen make good her threat?

Eventually his thoughts were interrupted by the arrival of an itinerant tinker, who came into the tavern complaining noisily of the weather. Benedict, disturbed by the other man's voice, looked up with a start, and then beckoned the landlord. "What's o'clock?" he asked abruptly.

"Close on two in the afternoon, your Honour."

"So late? I had best begone." He rose to his feet, slung his cloak about him, and on a sudden impulse tossed his one remaining gold piece on to the table. The man looked at it with starting eyes, but Benedict brushed past him and went out to fetch his horse from the ramshackle stable, wondering with profound self-mockery just what that arrogant gesture was supposed to have proved. A gauntlet thrown down to fate, perhaps? A defiance of whatever nameless power had spoken through Bronwen's lips? A declaration that the wealth of Monksfield would be his and that he would hold it in the teeth of any enemy who threatened him?

The weather was no less forbidding now than it had been earlier. Mist still covered the countryside like a pall, and the trees were black, frozen skeletons looming through it; his horse's breath rose in clouds on the icy air as though the beast were a dragon breathing smoke, and the ringing of its hooves on the frosty ground was the only sound to break the silence. It was like riding through a dead world, and an unaccountable sense of foreboding took possession of him.

The walls of Monksfield were already looming dimly before him when he heard a familiar whistled signal from somewhere on his right, and then Joseph's low voice, speaking in the lingua franca of the Barbary coast, warning him to wait. With his foreboding of disaster hardening to certainty, he drew rein and answered softly in the same tongue.

The servant materialised out of the mist beside him. "Master, praise be to Allah that I have found you! You are walking into a trap."

Swiftly, but with all a Muslim's imagery, he described what had taken place, and Benedict, listening to him, knew that his instinct of danger had not lied.

This was the one thing he had not foreseen, the contingency he had made no plans to deal with. It was hard to believe that Giles Aldon had never abandoned the hunt for Bronwen, and almost incredible that he had succeeded in tracking her to Monksfield, yet it was a fact. Aldon was here, and the peril which Benedict had sworn to her would never threaten her again had reached out to engulf her.

He was aware that Joseph had paused and was waiting expectantly for him to speak, but he could not. He could not even think. His mind was filled with pictures of Bronwen trapped again by the terror of the witch-hunt. His imagination, leaping ahead into the future, saw her flung into some pest-ridden gaol; stripped and shamed before a gaping crowd; dragged to the gallows through a howling mob that cried "death to the witch!" In a few brief, bitter moments he faced the truth, and knew that Monksfield mattered not at all; that the riches of the whole world would be meaningless to him if Bronwen died.

Joseph said tentatively: "Master, we should not linger so near to the house."

"No." Benedict roused himself with an effort. "Come away while I consider what is to be done. The spinney yonder will give us cover."

He wheeled his horse, and with Joseph loping along beside him, grasping the stirrup, came in a minute or two to the spinney, a thick tangle of young trees and undergrowth, with a few older, larger trees scattered through it. Beneath one of these Benedict drew rein and dismounted.

"Did any see you leave the house?"

Joseph shook his head. "I was careful. As soon as I heard the other servants babbling that my mistress was accused of witchcraft, I made my way to the gallery above the hall, to see and hear for myself what was taking place. When they haled her off, I bethought me it was time to begone, lest it occur to them to question me. I paused only long enough to arm myself, and to secure the gold which was in my charge, and then came in search of you."

"You did well. We shall need the gold to make our escape, but it will not aid us to fetch the lady Bronwen out of her prison. Monksfield is not a gaol, with turnkeys who may be bribed."

He stood frowning, lost in thought, absently stroking the horse's glossy neck while his mind ranged to and fro, seeking a way to rescue Bronwen. The first shock had passed now; he was alert again, the shrewd, experienced fighter considering a plan of action.

Joseph shifted uneasily from one foot to the other. It was loyalty and devotion to Benedict which had brought him hurrying from the house, just as it had kept him in London to watch over Bronwen at Benedict's command. He had a Muslim's tolerant contempt for women, and though he would always treat his master's lady with deference, and serve her well, she mattered nothing to him except as a possession of Benedict's; and what he had heard Giles Aldon say of her had filled him with misgiving. For the first time in his life he ventured to question his master's actions.

"Lord, we should begone in all haste. I will run by your side until another horse can be procured."

"Begone?" Slowly Benedict raised his head to look at

him. He spoke softly, but anger was kindling in his eyes. "Begone, say you, when your mistress lies prisoner yonder, under threat of death?"

"Master, they say she is a witch . . . !" The words ended in a choking gasp as Benedict's hand shot out to close upon his throat. Struggling for breath, Joseph felt himself jerked forward, lifted until his toes barely touched the ground, and held so, with Benedict's dark eyes, ablaze with fury, glaring into his from only a few inches away.

"Let me hear those words but once more on your lips," the deep voice said with deadly quiet, and an undertone of menace that sent a shiver along Joseph's spine, "and, by this hand, they will be the last you utter this side of hell! She is no witch. It is a false charge brought against her by the Aldons to cover their own mistreatment of her."

He released his hold as suddenly as he had taken it, and Joseph stumbled and dropped to his knees. Benedict stood looking down at him.

"You have served me faithfully for many years," he went on, "but unless you are prepared to give a like loyalty to your mistress, our ways part here. You will no longer be servant of mine."

"No, lord, no!" Joseph's voice was hoarse and strangled, but vehement with entreaty. "Do not send me away! Allah be my witness that I meant no harm."

"You will serve the lady Bronwen as faithfully as you serve me?"

"Master, I will. By the beard of the Prophet I swear it!"

"You accept my word that she is no witch?"

"She is no witch," Joseph repeated obediently. "The charge is false."

"And you will use every endeavour, risking your life if need be, to deliver her from her present danger?" Benedict demanded sternly.

"I will do anything, master, as long as I may continue to serve you."

"Very well. Get up, then, and let us consider how this may be done."

Joseph scrambled up, and stooped to brush the mud and dead leaves from his knees. "An ambush upon the road, master," he suggested, "when Colonel Aldon takes the lady Bronwen hence?"

Benedict shook his head. "Aldon is a soldier. If I do not return, he will guess that I have got wind of his presence and will take precautions against attack. If he carries Cromwell's authority he can command whatever aid he may need, and will not risk bringing her forth until he has an adequate escort." He paused, frowning, tapping his fingers thoughtfully on the hilt of his sword. "No, if I am to have her out of the house, I must return to it myself."

Joseph looked aghast. "Lord, you will be made prisoner."

"That is a risk I must take. From what you tell me, it would seem that Aldon is prepared, for some reason, to give me the benefit of the doubt, and to regard me as the victim of the lady Bronwen's supposed magic arts. I want to learn why. Devil knows he has no cause to love me."

"You will trust your life to that, master?"

"To that, and to my own wits. Also to the fact that

my uncle will not, I think, wish to believe me guilty, and so will not suffer me to be too rudely used in his house. But, whatever the outcome, I must go back to find her. Do you know where they have imprisoned her?"

"Master, Sir Nicholas told them to confine her in the moat cellar, if you know where that may be."

Benedict stared at the servant without really seeing him. He knew only too well. The present house of Monksfield had been raised upon the foundation of a much earlier manor, and the labyrinth of ancient passages and underground chambers on which it stood, dignified now by the name of cellars, had once served a harsher purpose. They were dungeons, where the very stones seemed steeped in misery; and the place known as the moat cellar was the worst of them all. On the lowest level, and adjacent to the remaining stretch of the moat, its slimy walls oozed constantly with water which collected in stagnant pools on the uneven floor, and no glimmer of daylight had ever penetrated its dank darkness.

The fact that Sir Nicholas had committed Bronwen to so horrible a prison was a measure of his conviction that she was indeed a witch, and showed Benedict how difficult would be the task of rescue. At the same time, the thought of her alone and terrified in that black, evil hole awoke in him a cold flame of anger against his uncle, against Aldon, against all who had a hand in her persecution. It was a flame banked down and as yet slow-burning, but all the more dangerous for that.

"We waste time," he said curtly. "Time enough to think of winning out of the house once I am inside it, and meanwhile we must secure our retreat. Horses will be our most urgent need."

"I could hire them from the inn in the village," Joseph suggested.

"Too risky! If it were discovered who you are, our race would be run before it had begun. Besides, the nags they are likely to have for hire will not be fleet enough, for if we are pursued, our pursuers' mounts will come from my uncle's stables." He broke off, and a grim smile touched his lips. "And so shall ours. We will have your own horses out before I go back to the house."

"From the stables here?" Joseph said blankly. "Master, have you forgotten Sir Nicholas's servants?"

Benedict shook his head. "I'll wager they are all within the house, gossiping over what has happened. Such excitement does not come their way once in a dozen years." He tethered his own horse to a low branch, and took off his cloak to spread it over the animal's back. "We'll go on foot. Come!"

He set off through the spinney, and Joseph followed with the fatalistic calm of his religion and his race. He believed that they were walking deliberately into disaster, but Benedict's judgment proved sound. The stables, stealthily approached, were empty of human life, and they were able to saddle both the horses, Bronwen's fleet white gypsy pony and Joseph's grey gelding, without being discovered. There was a thick, rough cloak hanging on a peg on the harness-room wall, and Benedict took that, too, and threw it across the pony's back.

The most dangerous part of the enterprise came when they had to lead the horses out of the stable and across the yard to the gate, for then the chance of discovery was greatest. Joseph led both beasts, and Benedict followed with his drawn sword in his hand, but the doors of Monksfield were fast shut against the cold, and no doubt the excited voices of the servants crowding the kitchen quarters served to drown any sound they made. They came undetected to the park again, and halted only when the drifting mist had hidden them from the house.

"Fetch my horse from the spinney," Benedict said then, "and take all three to the wood on the north side of the park. There is a hut there that the woodcutters use in due season. It is deserted now, and will serve to shelter and conceal the beasts until we need them. Wait with them until dusk, but if we come not by then, make your way to the gatehouse and enter it by stealth, concealing yourself somewhere within. I do not want to break free of the house only to waste precious moments seeking to open barred gates."

"Trust me, master. What of the gatekeeper?"

"He is old and lives alone, and you should not find it difficult to overpower him. Try not to harm him. We do not want to stir up more trouble than we must. How are you armed?"

"With pistols, master, and with this." He pulled aside his doublet to show the heavy Moorish dagger in a sheath strapped about his waist.

Benedict nodded his approval, for he knew how skilful Joseph was with that knife. His own pistols were in their holsters on his saddle, since of habit he never went unarmed upon even the shortest journey, and his sword was at his side. They were as well prepared as they could hope to be.

"Away with you, then, and await our coming."

Joseph bowed. It did not occur to him to doubt that coming, for he had implicit faith in his master's ability to accomplish what he set out to do. Only one minor point was troubling him.

"What if it is remarked, master, that though you rode away from the house, you returned on foot?"

"I shall say that my horse cast a shoe, and I left him at the smithy. Away, now!"

Joseph was satisfied. "May the protection of Allah be over you, master, and over the lady Bronwen," he said piously, and led the horses away towards the spinney.

Benedict watched them until they were swallowed up by the mist, and then set off briskly towards the house.

•   •   •   •   •

The first thing Benedict heard when he thrust open Monksfield's great door, was a voice he did not know expounding the dangers of witchcraft. He let the door close as it had opened, silently upon well-greased hinges, and stood for a few moments listening, himself hidden from the occupants of the hall by the carved screens.

The voice was level and unemotional, with a curious flatness of tone which robbed it of all feeling, so that the enormity of the things it was saying took several seconds to sink into its hearers' minds. The speaker, it seemed, had devoted considerable time to the study of

184

witches, their crimes, their detection and their ultimate fate, and when Benedict entered he was describing the trial and execution of the woman known as "the Witch of Wapping," who had been hanged some eighteen months previously.

Until that moment, Benedict had been inclined to regard Giles Aldon as an opportunist, prepared to use an accusation of witchcraft to rid his family of the embarrassment of Bronwen's existence, but as he listened to that cold, flat voice he knew beyond all doubt that the man believed what he was saying. In his eyes, Bronwen had sold herself to the Devil, and was guilty of everything of which she had been accused.

He went forward, round the screens. The occupants of the hall were grouped about the fire. Sir Nicholas hunched in his great chair, his head bowed, his hands lying limply on the carved wooden arms, Edith facing him with Mercy on a low stool at her side. The girl's face was buried in her hands, but Edith was leaning forward with an air of eagerness which Benedict found oddly repellent, her gaze fixed on the fourth member of the group, who stood between her and Sir Nicholas, facing the fire.

Aldon stopped speaking and turned as the newcomer's footsteps rang on the stone floor, and Benedict saw, in the pale, cruel face and light blue eyes, confirmation of what the voice had told him. There would be no mercy for Bronwen from this man, while the fact that he was apparently prepared to practise forbearance towards Benedict himself was more puzzling than before, and vaguely disquieting.

Sir Nicholas raised his head, and spoke in a voice

utterly unlike his usual bluff tones. "Nephew, this gentleman is Colonel Aldon. No doubt you can guess why he is here."

"I can guess!" To save his life Benedict could not have kept the contempt from his voice. "He is here to pursue his family's vengeful persecution of a wronged and defenceless girl."

The faintest tinge of colour crept into Aldon's pallid cheeks. "I am here to lay an accursed witch by the heels, and to see that she suffers just punishment for her crimes. Murderess and whore and servant of the Devil, she will most surely hang, and I would advise you, sir, to have a care that you are not implicated in her guilt."

Benedict, standing beside him, studied him for a moment without speaking, and the colour deepened a little in Aldon's face. Being of barely medium height, he preferred to stand while others sat, thus giving himself a sense of superiority, but now Benedict Forde was towering over him, a full head and shoulders taller than he, and it was that, as much as the barely veiled contempt in the dark eyes, which stung Giles Aldon to anger. Benedict's next words did nothing to appease him.

"So she will hang, will she? I perceive that Colonel Aldon is not merely the catchpoll, but judge and jury also. Her trial is already over."

His voice, with its infinite variations of expression, its power to say so much more than the mere words it spoke, was a weapon against which Aldon had no immediate defence. His self-esteem writhed under the lash of it, and it was small consolation to think of the power he could wield by virtue of his own rank and the authority of General Cromwell.

"Benedict!" Sir Nicholas spoke anxiously, almost beseechingly. "When you consorted with this woman, you did not—you could not have known that she is a witch?"

"I knew she was accused of it. I knew also that she is guilty of nothing save of being the loved foster-child of a rich man—and that is a crime only in the eyes of his avaricious kinfolk."

"What proof have you of her innocence?" Giles Aldon put in slyly. "What proof, sir, apart from her word?"

Benedict glared at him, but could find no answer. What proof could there be to set against evidence which he regarded as utterly incredible, but which to others was undeniable proof of Bronwen's guilt? In the face of superstition that believed witches capable of anything, from calling up storms at sea to causing the living flesh of their enemies to rot from their bones, what hope had reason and logic?

"You see?" the Colonel continued, with a smile which moved his lips but did not reach his eyes. "There *is* no proof of her innocence, but proof in plenty of her guilt. She chose to leave my brother's house to dwell in the one-time home of a proven witch. She cherished an imp in the shape of a rabbit, and therewith caused my nephew's death. She is known to bear the Devil's mark upon her body. And of that last fact, Mr Forde," he added with deliberate malice, "you must surely be aware."

"I do not deny such knowledge," Benedict replied

187

calmly, "but I tell you that this so-called Devil's mark is no more than an accident of birth."

"No doubt," Aldon snapped. "The mark of a witch-brood, Devil-begotten. Her mother, it is said, bore it also. And just as the mother wrought by magic arts upon my misguided kinsman, so the daughter, Mr Forde, has wrought upon you."

"Magic arts?" Benedict repeated, and laughed. "I cannot answer for your kinsman, Aldon, but I give you my word that Bronwen used no spells or charms to lure me. Nor needed to, with *her* beauty of face and body."

For a few seconds Aldon regarded him, and then turned to their companions, lifting his shoulders in an eloquent shrug. "My friends, what more is needed?" he said simply. "How could any man see beauty in that skinny, white-faced, green-eyed daughter of Satan unless his eyes were blinded by witchcraft? Even so did she bewitch my poor nephew before she murdered him."

Benedict looked from one to the other. They were all staring at him—Sir Nicholas with a mixture of disappointment and anger, Mercy with fearful curiosity, Edith with triumph tempered by disgust—but all with unquestioning acceptance of Aldon's words. Last of all he looked at Aldon himself, and knew beyond all doubt that nothing he could say would make the smallest impression on the man's absolute certainty of Bronwen's guilt. In his eyes she was a proven witch, and he would not rest until she had paid the ultimate penalty.

He fought down the futile anger against their blind

superstition that seethed within him, but found he could not subdue an insidious fear. As it was here, so it would be at whatever travesty of a trial they might subject Bronwen to; the verdict was a foregone conclusion. There was only one way to save her, and that was somehow to get her out of Suffolk; out of England, if that were possible. If he could lull Aldon's suspicions a little, make the Colonel believe that he was pinning his hopes on an acquittal once she was brought to trial, it might be done.

"We waste time," he said curtly. "I am not obliged, Aldon, to answer to you. I will give my evidence to her judges in due season, so, if you mean to take her hence, let us begone with no more delay."

Aldon shook his head. "It grows late, and darkness will come early tonight. Your good uncle bids me bide here until morning, and that we shall do. The witch is securely imprisoned."

With a tremendous effort Benedict bit back the angry protest that rose to his lips. It did not surprise him that Giles Aldon intended to leave Bronwen imprisoned all night in the moat cellar, but could she survive so many hours in the black, icy damp of that lightless hole? Even if she did, she would be in no case by morning to attempt escape. As he thought of what she had already suffered there, and must continue to suffer, his anger became almost too great to control. No sign of that inward struggle, however, was visible in his face, and Giles Aldon never knew that death was scarcely a heartbeat away.

"As for you, Mr Forde," the Colonel was saying, "it will be safer, I think, if you, too, are kept under some restraint. We are not dealing here with an ordinary crime."

Sir Nicholas looked up. "My nephew shall not be made a prisoner in my house, Colonel Aldon. Will not his word be enough?"

"With respect, Sir Nicholas, I think not. In any other circumstances I would readily accept Mr Forde's parole, but in this case . . . !" He paused apologetically. "Who can tell what powers that accursed woman, even though she is now exposed and imprisoned, may still exert over one whom she has bound with her devilish arts? For his own sake, your nephew should allow himself to be placed in custody."

Benedict gave a short, angry laugh, but Sir Nicholas appeared to see the force of this argument, and nodded solemn agreement. Edith looked complacent, no doubt expecting Aldon to demand that Benedict be thrust into the cellars as Bronwen had been, but her spite was not to be satisfied to that extent.

"I have no wish to cause Mr Forde more discomfort than is necessary," the Colonel continued smoothly. "It will be enough, I think, if he retires to his chamber, though I would ask, Sir Nicholas, that a watch be kept outside his door, as it is being kept outside the place where the woman is confined. It is not uncommon for an imprisoned witch to be visited by her imps and familiars, and it might be that she could despatch one of those demons to summon Mr Forde to her aid."

"A good thought," Sir Nicholas agreed heavily. "I will leave the ordering of the matter, sir, to you." He turned to Benedict. "I must ask you, nephew, to retire as Colonel Aldon requests. This is a grievous business!

I fear your roving in heathen lands, and your turning away from the paths of righteousness, has caused you to fall an easy victim to this woman's evil powers. Pray, nephew, that you may through the Lord's mercy find salvation. Wrestle with the forces of evil, repent of your sins, and you may yet win a place among the Lord's elect."

Aldon looked curiously at Benedict. "So Mr Forde has travelled in heathen lands! So, too, in his youth, did my kinsman, Sir Edwin Aldon, whom Bronwen's mother bewitched into giving her hell-begotten brat a home, and those travels prompted him to delve into secret arts and forbidden mysteries. Truly it is a fearful thing when the seeds of blasphemy fall upon fertile ground!"

Benedict said nothing. Words alone could not relieve the hell of anger and contempt raging within him, and if he let his fury find expression in premature action, Bronwen's fate would be sealed. He turned sharply away and strode across the hall and up the stairs, leaving Aldon to follow or not, as he chose.

•   •   •   •   •

The Colonel chose to follow. Benedict heard the footsteps coming after him, hurrying to catch up with his own long stride, but he did not pause until he reached his bedchamber. He went straight in, slamming the door in Aldon's face, and walked across to the window, where he stood staring out at the dreary, mist-enshrouded prospect beyond and wondering how he could rescue Bronwen from her guarded prison and escape from Monksfield without rousing the household. He did not shrink from the possibility of violent action—in his present frame of mind he would readily have taken on every man in the house—but stealth must be his first consideration. Escape from the house would be only the beginning, and after such rigorous imprisonment he could not tell whether or not Bronwen would be equal to the hard and headlong ride which would be necessary if pursuers were at their heels.

He had expected Aldon to follow him into the room, but time passed and he did not come. Benedict smiled grimly to himself. Perhaps, he thought, the Colonel did not relish the prospect of being alone with his prisoner.

This suspicion was presently confirmed. After a time, the door opened and Benedict turned to see Aldon coming in, followed by a servant who certainly did not belong to Monksfield. The man closed the door and remained standing by it while Aldon advanced into the room.

"As you are aware, Mr Forde," he remarked, "Sir Nicholas has entrusted the task of securing you to me and to the servants who accompany me. I must therefore ask you to render up your sword."

Benedict looked from him to the servant by the door. The man, he noticed, carried a pistol thrust into his belt, and there was a coil of rope slung over his arm.

"As you will," he said with a shrug, and lifted the baldrick over his head. Aldon took the sheathed weapon, and beckoned the servant forward.

"There is a bolt on the inside of yonder door," He

said, "but none on the outside, and there is no key. I regret, therefore, that it will be necessary to bind you. Be good enough to place your hands behind your back."

This was something Benedict had not expected. Coolly and deliberately he estimated the chances of overcoming both Aldon and the servant before they could overpower him, decided the odds were against him, and did as he was asked. The servant lashed his wrists together and his arms to his sides; when that was done, Aldon, who had watched in silence, holding Benedict's sheathed sword cradled in the crook of his arm, said unemotionally:

"Now pray sit down. It is necessary to bind your legs also and I have no wish to cause you greater discomfort than is needful."

"You are all consideration, sir," Benedict replied ironically, walking across to the bed and sitting down on the edge of it. "I am led to hope that you will even provide me with supper."

"By all means, sir. My own men shall bring it to you." Aldon paused, watching the servant who was now kneeling at Benedict's feet and fastening his bonds with brisk efficiency. "They will, of course, be armed," he added as an afterthought.

Benedict made no reply. The servant fastened the last knot and rose to his feet, to be handed the sword and then dismissed by a curt gesture. As the door closed behind him Aldon said abruptly:

"You are no doubt wondering how I contrived to find you and the woman. When you carried her off into the forest you vanished so successfully that all our efforts to discover you met with failure. You would have escaped altogether but for your chance encounter with my brother's servant, Thomas Barnes, and the greed which led you to attack and rob him."

He paused to study the effect of his words, but no flicker of emotion crossed the gaunt, dark face confronting him. Benedict looked back at him with complete indifference, and when the Colonel spoke again, his voice had lost an infinitesimal part of its smoothness.

"Barnes had not the wit to connect his misfortune with the witch, but when he spoke of his meeting with you at the inn, I was struck by the similarity between his description of you, and that of the man who rescued her. I took the trouble to visit the inn myself, and learned from the landlord's wife that you had a woman with you that day who could be none other than Bronwen herself, and that you were bound for London. After that it was simply a matter of patience, and of employing a sufficient number of men to search for you." He paused, and once again his lips moved in that humourless smile which did not reach his eyes. "Neither you nor she is of an appearance which passes unnoticed."

Benedict did not allow himself to betray the chagrin he felt—he would not give Aldon that satisfaction— but he realised how greatly he had underestimated the man. If it had occurred to him at all that the attack on Thomas Barnes might be connected with him, he had dismissed it with the thought that once he and Bronwen had vanished into the teeming heart of the city they would be safe from any pursuit. He had reckoned without the tenacity of purpose Giles Aldon obviously possessed.

"You will notice," Aldon resumed after a moment, "that I have not yet accused you of that robbery, or permitted you and Barnes—who is here with me—to meet, but rest assured that if I do accuse you, you will be tried and convicted. And highway robbery, let me remind you, is a hanging matter."

He paused again to let these words sink in. Benedict looked blandly back at him, but behind that impassive mask his mind moved swiftly, probing for the reason for Aldon's apparent magnanimity. The man seemed strangely anxious to believe that Benedict's association with Bronwen was due to her use of the black arts, and not to his own free will.

"Since my arrival here," Aldon continued, "I have learned that you are your uncle's heir, and the future husband of Miss Mercy. A goodly prospect, Mr Forde! Do you mean to let it slip through your fingers?"

Benedict's brows lifted. "That, sir, surely depends upon you."

"On the contrary! It depends upon you." He moved closer and lowered his voice. "Bear witness against the witch, help me to send her to the gallows, and no more shall be said of the waylaying of Thomas Barnes or the gold of which he was robbed."

So that was it! Aldon was so eager for Bronwen's death, so obsessed by his conviction of her guilt, that he was even prepared to overlook the theft of five hundred pounds, if by doing so he could make her fate more certain. Yet why did he think it necessary?

"Do you need my help?" Benedict asked ironically. "You have said that she will surely hang."

"If there is justice to be had, she will, but of late there have been those—men of learning, more shame to them—who seek to discredit belief in the existence of witches, even in the face of Holy Writ itself. There must be no doubt of this woman's fate. She *must* die, for only by death can her power be broken."

For the first time, feeling sounded in his voice, an oddly repellent mixture of hatred and fear, and Benedict, looking curiously at him, saw the same emotions mirrored in the pale, cold eyes. He was puzzled. There was something more here than a mere fanatical hatred of witchcraft.

"The witch must die," Aldon repeated in the same indescribable tone. "Hark you, Mr Forde! Before she left my brother's house, she laid a curse upon him and upon all our family, that the name of Aldon shall perish and be known no more. Already it has begun. My nephew Francis is dead. My brother has but one other son, Mark, who in his turn has an only son, a child now four years old. Two weeks since, Mark's wife gave birth to her second child—a stillborn boy. My own children, to my sorrow, are all girls. The curse *must* be lifted! That accursed daughter of evil must be destroyed."

Benedict's thoughts leapt back to the day when he and Bronwen had met, and to what she had told him of her prophecy to Sir John. "It will come to pass," she had said, and if he had doubted then, he doubted no longer. Had she not similarly foreseen this moment, and Benedict himself, in bonds, confronting an enemy who held over him the power of life or death?

"And for that," he said slowly, "you need my help?"

Aldon nodded. "I must be certain that she has no hope of escape. To be plain with you, your evidence will carry weight, upon whichever side you choose to give it. As I have said, there are those who seek to prove that witches do not exist, and it may be that some will say that I and my brother are moved by self-interest in seeking the death of this woman. We do not lack for enemies."

"And are you not?" Benedict asked dryly. "Is it not self-interest to seek to lift the curse you believe she has laid upon you?"

"Perhaps," Aldon agreed coldly, "Just as you will serve your own interests by aiding me to destroy her evil power. Has she not placed your future in jeopardy by following you here? Your interests and mine are bound together in this." He drew a step nearer, and now there was impatience in his voice. "Well, Forde, which is it to be? An ignominious death upon the gallows for highway robbery, or a prosperous and respected life here at Monksfield, free at last of the web of evil this woman has spun about you?"

Benedict shifted himself, with difficulty, into a more comfortable position. His dark eyes met the Colonel's pale ones with bland indifference.

"What choice do I have? I will bear witness, so now loose me these bonds."

A look of satisfaction came into Aldon's face, but he shook his head. "No, I think not. I rejoice that the Lord has opened your eyes to the true depths of this

197

woman's evil, but for your own sake it is better that you remain confined. I have curbed her power by making her prisoner and depriving her of the means to use her spells and incantations, but the danger may not yet be past. Better to endure a trifling discomfort now than to imperil your immortal soul when it has just been snatched from Satan's greedy claws."

From this resolve no argument could move him. He advised Benedict to spend the hours of the night in prayer, and in spiritual wrestling with the powers of darkness which still hovered so dangerously close, and then left him alone. Having closed the door behind him, he was arrested in the act of turning away by the sound of the prisoner's voice speaking again within the room, but a moment's attentive listening informed him that this was not raised in prayer. In point of fact Benedict was cursing, deeply and quietly and with profound feeling, but since, finding mere English inadequate, he had reverted to the more colourful language of the Barbary coast, it sounded to Colonel Aldon inexpressibly evil. He muttered a prayer himself, and hurried away.

Part Seven

Bronwen, thrust roughly into the darkness of her prison, had stumbled and fallen to hands and knees as the door slammed shut. The shock of the fall, and the abrupt withdrawal of all light and sound, dazed and bewildered her, so that by the time she staggered to her feet she had lost all sense of direction, and blundered forward until her outstretched hands collided with the wall of her cell, with stone which oozed water and was slimy with fungus. She cried out and, recoiling, slipped in a pool of icy water and went down again. The horror of the place, the total darkness and the dripping stone, the walls which seemed to be closing in upon her, brought her to the verge of panic, so that she groped wildly to and fro, sobbing with terror. She had the feeling of being entombed alive, of having been thrust into utter oblivion from which she would never again emerge into light and air and human company.

It was finding the door which saved her from complete hysteria. For what seemed an eternity she had been groping around the walls, bruising herself against them, stumbling in puddles which soaked her shoes and the lower edges of her skirts, until it seemed that she must be mad, that the door through which she had been thrust into this awful place had vanished, enclosing her completely in slimy, dripping stone. Then, suddenly, it was there beneath her fingertips; the different texture of damp wood, the hard protrusions of the iron with which it was studded. Fumbling blindly across it, she discovered at about the level of her face a small, barred opening, closed on the outside by some kind of shutter yet indicating, by its very existence, the presence beyond it of living men and women. She clung to the bars, pressing herself against the door, straining her ears until she thought she could catch, now and then, the faint sound of voices.

For a long time she stood there, gripping the iron bars, but slowly the icy chill of the cellar crept through her, penetrating, it seemed, her very bones. Her hands grew numb and slipped from their hold, and she slid down to crouch at the foot of the door, huddling her limbs together to try to combat the all-pervading cold.

Disjointed pictures drifted through her mind. Of Giles Aldon's light, cruel eyes blazing with triumph as she was dragged away; of Edith, shocked, frightened yet morbidly eager to hear every detail of her supposed crimes; of Thomas Barnes, his mere presence recalling that earlier horror, the cruel witch-hunt from which

200

Benedict had saved her. Of suffering still to be endured; the public examination and trial, the inevitable death-sentence, and its execution which the mob would turn into a macabre festival. This time there was no way of escape, no chance of a swift, merciful, self-inflicted death. She was young and healthy. There was no reason to suppose she would not survive every hardship until the hangman put an end to suffering for ever.

And Benedict? She tried not to think of him, not to remember all they had been to each other and could never be again, for in her present hopeless plight such thoughts brought pain sharper even than her fear of what lay ahead. Harder to bear, though, than either fear or pain, was self-reproach for the disaster she had brought upon him. If only she had not come to Monksfield. If Colonel Aldon had found her in London there was a chance that Benedict need not have been implicated. He might have stayed in Suffolk, married his cousin, become a rich and respected landowner. Her prophetic powers had played her false, showing her only one glimpse of the future, one side of the coin. Benedict's danger, but not her own; his enemy, who in fact was hers; the enemy into whose hands she had unwittingly delivered him, whom she would have given her own life to protect.

Yet, had she? Giles Aldon had made no accusation against him, had seemed inclined to regard him with sympathy, even to the length of suggesting that he had been the helpless victim of witchcraft. If that belief could be encouraged, if she could convince her ac-cusers that she had ensnared Benedict by use of the black arts, so that everything that happened had been by her will and not by his . . .

That should not be too difficult to accomplish. Once a woman was accused of witchcraft, any crime, however far-fetched, might be laid at her door. The only obstacle was Benedict himself. She knew he would not stand aside and let such charges be brought against her. He would fight by every means in his power as long as he thought there was the smallest chance of saving her, not seeing that she had been doomed from the moment Giles Aldon arrived at Monksfield.

She was so numbed, physically and mentally, by the cold and the despair, that it was a long time before the obvious solution presented itself, but when it did, she knew that she must carry it out at once, before resolution had time to falter. It was the only way to save him, but in taking it she must extinguish even the tiny flicker of hope which burns in every human soul as long as life remains. She dragged herself up, and began to pound on the door with her fists, hoping that those who had been ordered to keep watch outside her prison were faithful to their duty.

At first her attempts to attract attention brought no response, but at last the shutter was forced aside and the feeble rays of the lantern penetrated the blackness of the cellar. Faint though it was, the light dazzled her so that she had to cover her eyes with her hands, but she sensed someone peering at her through the bars. Then the familiar, hated voice of Thomas Barnes said roughly:

"Quit that noise, you hell-hag, or you will suffer for it."

Bronwen raised her head, blinking painfully. "Take me again before your master," she demanded. "'I must speak with him."

"'Must', she says!" Barnes mocked her, evidently for the benefit of an unseen companion. "Still so haughty, are you, thinking I must do your bidding? You'll bide where you are, wench, until the Colonel pleases to send for you."

"Wait!" Bronwen said desperately, fearing that he was about to close the shutter again. "At least carry word to him. Tell him I will make confession."

"Try to trick me, would you?" Barnes retorted. "Have me bring you forth so that you can summon your Devil's imps to your aid . . . !" He broke off, peering more closely through the bars. "Confession, say you?"

"Yes, yes! Confession to all his charges. Go to him, I beg you! He would not thank you for refusing me."

"That's the truth, at all events," Barnes muttered. He hesitated, and then turned away. The shutter scraped back into its place, but before it closed completely Bronwen heard him say: "Keep close watch, friend, for this may be some Devil's trick. I'm for the Colonel."

There followed another period of darkness and silence and nerve-racking anxiety, and then at last bolts scraped and the door creaked open. Barnes and another man stood on the threshold, silhouetted against the lantern-light.

"Come out, witch!" Barnes said roughly. "The Colonel waits your coming."

Bronwen stumbled forward, so stiff and numb with

cold that she could scarcely walk. Barnes laid hold of her with deliberate cruelty and, commanding the other man to go first with the lantern, half dragged, half carried her through the passages and up the steps.

In the hall, Giles Aldon and Sir Nicholas Forde were waiting by the fire. Edith was there, too, in the background, but of Mercy there was now no sign. Candles had been lit, for darkness was gathering beyond the windows, and Bronwen realised with a sense of dull surprise that she must have been imprisoned for several hours.

For perhaps a minute Giles Aldon studied her without speaking, taking grim satisfaction in the changes in her appearance since last they stood face to face. Bronwen's violet riding-dress was patched with damp and stained with smears of green slime from the stones of the moat cellar. Her hands were bruised and bleeding, and her face white and drawn and pinched with cold; she swayed on her feet, so that Barnes's grip on her arm was necessary as a support rather than to restrain her. Aldon saw in all this evidence of a broken spirit, and his lips broadened a fraction in his mirthless smile.

"There is nothing so effective as a taste of prison to chasten a rebellious spirit," he said at last in his flat, unfeeling voice. "I am told you are now ready to confess your crimes."

Bronwen had been standing with bowed head, her whole attention concentrated on the effort needed to remain on her feet, but the sneering words stung her pride and acted upon her like a strong restorative. She raised her head and looked at him, and there was that in her strange, green, slanted eyes which gave the lie to all he had been thinking, and pierced him with a cold blade of fear.

"I confess to being a witch," she said in a low, clear voice. "By witchcraft I killed Francis Aldon, and by witchcraft, although he knows it not, I drew unto me Benedict Forde, binding him with the chains of desire by means of the power I have of the Devil. And by witchcraft, Giles Aldon, I have sealed the doom of your house and encompassed its destruction. Hang me if you will. Satan my master will terribly avenge my death."

．　　　　．　　　　．　　　　．　　　　．

Benedict's loss of temper, the anger which was directed as much against himself as against Aldon because he had once more underestimated the man, did not for long deflect him from his purpose. Even while he relieved his feelings with curses, he was cautiously testing the strength of his bonds.

The rope was far from new, but even so, Aldon had not been careless and it would have held most men securely enough, but in some ways Benedict Forde was no ordinary man. Colonel Aldon had no conception of the enormous strength of his arms and back and shoulders; strength hard-won in the pitiless hell of the galleys, born of the endless hours of toiling, for month after month, to thrust and haul with his fellow-slaves at a heavy, fifteen-foot oar. That strength he now put forth, again and again until the sweat streamed off him. Until at last the weakest strand of rope parted, and then another and another. Until the bonds slackened and dropped, and his arms were free.

He untied his legs and then rested for a minute or two, considering his next move. It had taken time to free himself, and already the sky was darkening. Nightfall was not far off, and Bronwen had been a prisoner since midday. How was she faring, alone in that grim hole deep in Monksfield's ancient foundations? How could he reach her without some member of the household seeing him and raising the alarm?

It was impossible to plan more than one step ahead, and his first task must be to deal with whatever guard had been set outside his door. He pulled off his boots, then, moving silently on stockinged feet, stole across to the door and with infinite care lifted the latch. Drawing the door open inch by cautious inch, he applied his eye to the crack and so discovered the servant who had bound him sitting in a chair set directly opposite, but by a stroke of good luck the man's arms were folded and his chin sunk on his chest. Benedict opened the door wide and stepped softly through.

Perhaps, in spite of his care, he made some slight sound, or perhaps it was merely the sense of another presence close by which roused the servant, but whatever the reason, his head jerked up and his eyes opened. They dilated with superstitious horror as he discovered the man whom he had left bound hand and foot, free and towering over him, but before he could utter a sound Benedict's clenched fist rose and fell, and the servant slumped down again in the chair. Benedict stooped, heaved the fellow up across his shoulder and carried him into the bedchamber, where the remains of his own bonds served to tie wrists and ankles, and a strip torn from the sheet was soon fashioned into a gag.

Benedict resumed his boots, tucked the servant's pistol into the top of one of them, and once more emerged from the room. His purpose now was to reach Bronwen as quickly as he could, but the usual entrance to the cellars, situated as it was in the domestic quarters, would be almost impossible to reach unobserved at this hour of the day, when the servants were busy preparing supper and would be coming and going between the kitchen and the dining-parlour. He had remembered, however, that in his boyhood there had been another entrance, seldom used, behind a door in the panelling of the old chapel of pre-Reformation days. This seemed to offer the best chance of success, even though to reach it he must descend the staircase and cross the hall. He might have to wait until Sir Nicholas and the others went in to supper, though if fortune favoured him they might now be in one or other of the parlours, and the hall deserted.

When he reached the gallery, however, he realised that he was not to be thus fortunate, for Giles Aldon's flat, toneless voice was speaking in the hall below. Benedict did not catch what he said, but the tone was interrogatory; there was a moment's pause, and then, unmistakably, Bronwen's voice replied.

So Aldon had brought her before him again for questioning. That might make the task of rescue simpler. The gallery was as yet unlighted, though candles were burning in the hall, and Benedict decided it would be safe to risk looking down to form some estimate of the odds against him. He moved stealthily forward, so intent on what was going on below that he stumbled over a shadowy figure kneeling beside the balustrade and peering down through the ornate carving.

The shock was mutual, but Benedict's reaction was a fraction quicker than the other's. In one swift movement he seized the dimly-seen figure in an iron grip, pinning its arms to its sides and clapping a hand across its mouth—and realising, even as he did so, that it was Mercy he held. He did not relax his hold, but bent his head until his lips almost brushed her ear and said in a whisper:

"Be still! You'll come to no harm unless you try to cry out."

Straightening up, he lifted her off her feet and carried her to the great square window above the porch, where the long, heavy curtains would hide them from anyone entering the gallery. Still in the same breath of a whisper, he said:

"I've no wish to hurt you. Have I your promise to make no sound?"

She nodded vigorously. He set her down on the seat which encircled the window, sat beside her and removed his hand from her mouth, but only to lower it to her throat. He tighted the grip a little, letting her feel the strength of his fingers.

"One squeak out of you, my child, and you'll not speak again these many hours," he warned her grimly. "Why were you skulking there?"

She swallowed hard. "Mother sent me away because they were bringing the witch before Colonel Aldon again. She told me to go to my chamber, but I wanted to hear what was said. Cousin, how did you . . .?"

"I broke my bonds," he interrupted curtly. "Mercy, listen to me! Bronwen is no witch. She is as innocent of any taint of witchcraft as you are yourself, but Aldon is determined upon her death. Nothing less will satisfy him. I mean to take her from him, and neither you nor any other shall stand in my way."

Mercy was staring at him, wide-eyed. "So you really do not know!" she whispered. "She said that you did not. Cousin, you are deceived in her. She has confessed her guilt."

She felt him stiffen as though she had dealt him a physical hurt. "Confessed?" he repeated incredulously. "To witchcraft?"

"To everything! To being a witch, and keeping an imp in the form of a rabbit. To killing that young man, and putting a curse on all his family. To ensnaring you by magic and bewitching you into believing her innocent. Even—even to carnal knowledge of the Devil."

"You are lying!" Involuntarily his grip on her tightened, so that she gave a little whimper of mingled fright and pain. "Lying, or—by God! What has he done to her to wring such false confession from her lips?"

"Nothing! Nothing at all, I promise you. Look down into the hall, and you will see that she has not been harmed. She demanded to be brought to him to make confession, and seems to glory in her own wickedness. Her servant and both the horses have vanished, and when the Colonel questioned her about that, she laughed, and said they were demons who had taken that shape but had now flown back to hell."

Benedict sat staring at her, doubting the evidence of

his senses. It was transparently clear that Mercy was not lying—it was doubtful, in fact, whether she was even capable of inventing some of the things she had told him—but what madness had possessed Bronwen to confess to such absurdities? To seal her own fate beyond the last faint hope of acquittal?

"She said that she came here because by her magical arts she had learned you were to marry me, and she meant to wed you herself," Mercy went on. "She would have been lady of Monksfield, she said, and no one would have been able to gainsay her, had it not been discovered that she is a witch. Then Grandfather begged her to free you from the spell by which she has bound you, but she would not. She said that only her death would loose it, and that you will believe in her and desire her until she has drawn her last breath."

Understanding came to Benedict like light falling suddenly into a darkened room. This was for him. For his sake Bronwen had confessed to every absurd charge Giles Aldon had flung at her, and even invented one or two of her own. To make them believe him her dupe, a helpless pawn held prisoner by the unholy powers of a witch. She had foreseen that he would deny it, would try to convince them of her innocence, so that now anything he said or did on her behalf would seem but added proof of her witch-hood. In memory he heard her saying, as she had said last night, "I would give my own life, if need be," and knew that she was doing exactly that. She had signed her own death-warrant so that he might live and prosper. That was the measure of her love for him.

With a stifled groan he buried his head in his hands, his fingers writhing deep into his thick black hair. What had he done that she should love him so? He had saved her, it was true, from the witch-hunt—and then seduced her. He had robbed for her, as any thief might do for his doxy—and by that robbery set Giles Aldon on her track again. He had left her in order to come scheming after his uncle's fortune and would have entered into an empty, loveless marriage to secure it—but with no thought of giving up Bronwen. He must possess her still, even though it meant hiding her away in shameful secrecy.

He had forgotten Mercy's presence, forgotten the need to hold her prisoner, forgotten, in fact, her very existence, as in an agony of self-loathing and self-abasement he faced, for the first time, the ugly truth, and recognised how worthless was the life that Bronwen was giving hers to save. He had believed in nothing, cared for nothing; denied both God and Devil; but now the process which had begun hours before when Joseph told him of her danger reached its climax, and for the first time in many years he found himself praying. Wordlessly, passionately, not to Christ or to Allah but to the supreme and merciful God who must surely exist in and beyond both. Silently offering up his own life, his own immortal soul, as the price of her freedom and her safety.

Mercy, loosed from his hold, totally forgotten, made no attempt to escape. Not insensitive, she was aware of his suffering without being able to understand it. Tentatively, compassionately, she laid her hand gently on his hunched shoulder, but he made not the slightest response, and she continued to sit helplessly beside him, not knowing what to say or to do, just listening to the indistinguishable murmur of voices, Aldon's and Bronwen's, in question and answer in the hall below.

A sudden loud knocking on the great door in the porch beneath them made her jump. There was urgency in it, a portent of momentous tidings, which penetrated even Benedict's absorption. He raised his head, frowning, and then rose and stepped silently to the balustrade to look down.

At first he was aware only of Bronwen, standing there alone and defiant; of her stained garments and the white weariness in her face. Of her complete and awful isolation, for Thomas Barnes, and another man who had apparently been guarding her, had drawn back, as though fearful of too close contact with a confessed servant of the Devil. Giles Aldon stood facing her, but he had paused in what he was saying to look towards the source of that urgent knocking, and the heads of Sir Nicholas and Edith, and of Barnes and his companion, were turned in the same direction. Only Bronwen stared straight before her, as though even the small effort needed to look round was beyond her strength.

One of Sir Nicholas's servants hurried to open the door, there was a brief murmur of question and answer, and then a man in the dress of an upper servant came round the screens. He was splashed with mud from shoulder to heel, and stumbled as he walked as though in the last extremity of exhaustion. Halting in front of Aldon, he dragged off his hat and tried to bow.

"Colonel!" His voice was hoarse with fatigue, but it reached clearly enough to the watcher in the gallery. "Praise the Lord I have found you at last. Lady Aldon sent me. I rode to London. Followed you here." He paused, as though trying to collect his wits, and brushed one hand across his eyes. "Grievous news, your Honour. Your brother, Sir John, is dead."

Aldon uttered an exclamation. Took a pace forward and gripped the messenger by the arm. "Dead?" he rapped. "How, man, and when?"

"Two nights since. A fire. A great fire, sir. The Hall is utterly destroyed. Mr Mark died, too, and his lady. She was still weak after her lying-in. Sir John went back, to try to save the little boy, but . . ." The man broke off, helplessly shaking his head.

"Mark's son, too?" Aldon repeated hoarsely. "No, not the child, too!"

The messenger nodded. "All of them, Colonel! Only her ladyship and the young ladies escaped—and a few of us servants. We tried to fight the blaze, but 'twas no use."

His knees buckled suddenly, and he would have fallen if Barnes had not sprung forward to support him, hooking a stool towards him with his foot and lowering the messenger on to it. In the gallery, Benedict stood as still as death. Mercy had come to his side; he was aware of it, aware of her shocked gasp, but only with the edge of consciousness. He was thinking of a summer nightfall in the forest, and of Bronwen's quiet voice saying, "I have seen it. New tombs in the

213

church, and cold grey ashes blowing down the wind." Her prophecy had been terribly fulfilled.

" 'Twas no use," the messenger was repeating foolishly. "We fought the flames till we dropped, and they burned but the fiercer. Fierce as the flames of hell itself."

"The flames of hell!" Aldon repeated in a strange, harsh voice. "The flames of hell!" His eyes turned towards Bronwen. "This was your doing, you Devil's hag! Yours and your accursed demons!"

As the words left his lips he sprang at her, his hands reaching for her throat. The force of the attack flung her against the long table in the middle of the hall. She was bent backwards across it, beating feebly at him with her bruised hands, and trying to tear the murderous fingers from her throat.

With Aldon's assault on Bronwen, the anger which for hours had been simmering beneath Benedict's superficial calm broke through at last, in a raging torrent that swept away every consideration of prudence and caution. The pistol was already in his hand, but all such weapons were inaccurate, and with one he did not know he dared not risk a shot so close to Bronwen. He leaned over the balustrade and loosed a great shout.

"Aldon! Coward! Poltroon! Do you fear to face a man?"

The Colonel let Bronwen go and spun round as though jerked by an invisible cord. For an instant he stared in disbelief, and then sprang towards the stairs, wrenching his sword from its scabbard. Benedict raised the pistol and fired, but the shot went wide, and a mo-

214

ment later he was racing along the gallery to meet his enemy.

He reached the head of the stairs as Aldon came pounding up the last broad flight. The Colonel's lips were drawn back in a grin of exultation at finding himself confronting an unarmed adversary, but Benedict's fury was such that the odds against him meant nothing. He paused, and hurled the empty pistol with all his strength. It struck Aldon full in the chest with a force which made him grunt and stumble, and before he could recover his balance Benedict was upon him. Aldon lunged wildly with his sword, but Benedict swayed aside from the desperate thrust and caught Aldon by the right wrist with one hand and the front of his leather buff-coat with the other. For a few seconds they swayed to and fro there at the head of the stairs, and then Aldon uttered a sharp cry of pain and the sword slipped from a suddenly useless hand to slide and clatter down half a dozen stairs before coming to rest.

Then the watchers in the hall below, and Mercy at the other end of the gallery, saw a thing they would not have believed possible. That they could never afterwards believe would have been possible to a man of ordinary human powers. They saw Giles Aldon gripped in Benedict's two hands; saw him lifted, in spite of his frantic struggles, clear off his feet, higher and higher until he was above the other man's head; saw him held there for a second and then hurled with terrific force over the balustrade to hurtle with a despairing shriek on to the stone flags twenty feet below. In the instant of utter silence which followed, one of the women screamed.

Benedict was already moving by the time Aldon struck the ground. He swooped on the fallen sword, snatched it up and came on down the stairs in great leaps. Thomas Barnes, recovering from his stupefaction, drew his own sword and ran to intercept him. There was a brief, fierce clash of steel and then Benedict raced on across the hall, leaving Barnes coughing out his life at the foot of the stairs.

He reached Bronwen, huddled on her knees by the table with her hands at her throat, and almost without a pause, or so it seemed, lifted her to her feet. Holding her with his left arm encircling her waist, he swept her back with him to the screens masking the door.

Other servants, drawn by the commotion, came crowding into the hall, to stare in horror at the two dead men, at Sir Nicholas bending over Aldon's broken body, and at Edith huddled shrieking in her chair by the fire. They saw, too, the perpetrator of this outrage, but not one of them ventured to approach him. It was not merely the naked, reddened sword in his hand, or the grim evidence of his prowess staining the stone floor, that held them in check. It was the fear of the supernatural. Colonel Aldon's servants had boasted that Benedict Forde was a bound and guarded prisoner, yet here he was, armed and invincible, with the witch drooping across his arm and two deaths already to his discredit. They might have overwhelmed him by sheer weight of numbers, but not one of them could summon up enough courage to make any move against one so clearly possessed by the Devil.

Seeing that he need have no fear of an immediate attack, Benedict retreated round the screens and out into the courtyard. Joseph, alerted by the noise, was already there, and hurried forward as his master emerged from the porch into the light of the torches which flared on either side of it.

"The wicket-gate is open, master, and the gatekeeper a prisoner." He looked at the drooping figure Benedict was supporting. "The lady Bronwen . . . ?"

"Not greatly harmed, thank God! Here, take this!" Benedict thrust the sword into Joseph's hand and swept Bronwen up into his arms, striding with her across the courtyard, Joseph at his heels. Once outside the gates, and with the wicket pulled shut behind them, he added: "Hurry ahead and fetch the horses. Bring them to that great oak tree at the edge of the wood."

Joseph hastened away at once, melting like a shadow into the mist, and Benedict followed more slowly. Bronwen said in a painful whisper:

"Set me down, Benedict. I am able to walk."

"Bide still." His arms tightened about her. "I would carry you all night, if need be."

She cast a fearful glance back across his shoulder. Here in the open it was still not quite dark, but already the walls of Monksfield were no more than a shadow in the misty dusk, unsubstantial as the ghost of a house.

"Will they follow us?"

"Not yet, I think. We have left enough fear and confusion behind us to delay pursuit, probably even until morning. The horses are nearby. We can be miles away by dawn."

She slid her arm around his neck, pressing her face into the hollow of his shoulder, and did not speak again until they reached the oak tree. There he did set her on her feet, but only to draw her close and kiss her, long and tenderly. Then, very gently, he touched her throat, where the high lace collar of her habit had been torn open, and Giles Aldon's fingers left angry red weals on the white skin.

"He hurt you," he said in a low voice. "My poor love, you have suffered so much today."

"It does not matter," she murmured, and then suddenly she was weeping quietly, with weariness, with reaction from her recent fears, with sorrow and remorse. "Benedict, forgive me! I have brought you nothing but trouble."

"Hush, sweetheart." He held her close, protectively, as a man will hold his dearest possession on earth. There was much he wanted to say to her, but this was not the time. "There *is* need of forgiveness between us, but you are not the one who should be asking it."

A horse snorted nearby, and then Joseph materialised again out of the mist, mounted on the grey and leading the other two animals. Benedict looked down at Bronwen.

"Can you ride, my heart, or shall I take you up before me, and let Joseph lead your horse?"

"I can ride." She drew a deep breath, and wiped the tears from her cheeks with her fingertips. "We shall make better time so, and our danger is not over yet."

*   *   *   *   *

The little fishing vessel was putting out to sea on the morning tide, thrusting her sturdy bows into the grey, foam-streaked waters of the North Sea before a freshening breeze. Benedict stood on her deck, with his back to the flat coastline of England now receding into the distance, and drew the first carefree breath of freedom. Now he could relax his vigilance for the first time in three anxious days; now, at last, he could be sure that Bronwen was safe.

Guessing that pursuit, when it came, would first turn directly seaward, he had not, on leaving Monksfield, made for the coast, but headed north, into the fen country. There the influence of Sir Nicholas Forde did not reach, and the fen-people, a fiercely independent race, were apt to deal kindly with fugitives. Nevertheless it had been an anxious time, of hurried moves from one refuge to another, of cautious seeking for a vessel to bear them overseas, for a captain who was prepared to let gold silence all questions. Still, they had met with success in the end, by representing themselves as Royalists fleeing into exile, which was a common enough happening in these troubled times.

It was good to be at sea again, to feel the familiar lift of a deck beneath his feet, and to taste the salt in the air; to know once more the sense of freedom and anticipation of adventure which always came to him at the start of a journey. The past weeks at Monksfield seemed, in retrospect, like a time of imprisonment, and though his own stubbornness, his inherent dislike of being turned from any purpose against his will, had made him cling to the prospect of inheritance, he was aware now of nothing except a sense of liberation, of a burden having been lifted from him.

He thought of Bronwen, below decks in the stuffy little cabin which was the only accommodation the vessel could offer. Now, perhaps, the haunted look would begin to fade from her eyes. It would be a long time before she forgot the horrors of the moat cellar, or the brief, fierce eruption of violence which had followed her imprisonment, but now, at least, forgetfulness could begin. They were bound first for Holland, but he intended to travel south through France and Italy, to lands so different from anything she had ever known that in time the perils she had passed through would seem like nothing more than the memory of an evil dream.

There was a light footfall behind him, and Bronwen herself came to stand at his side. The rough cloak he had taken from the harness-room at Monksfield still wrapped her about, for there had been no opportunity to purchase a better one, and she had refused to deprive him again of his. Between the coarse cloth and the midnight darkness of her hair, her face still showed white and drawn, with violet shadows beneath the eyes. He put his arm about her, holding her close beside him, but said with mock sternness: "I bade you rest."

She made a little grimace. "I fear I am a poor companion for a seafarer, for my heart misgives me, especially when I am shut below in the cabin. Besides, I wanted a last glimpse of England."

"No." Benedict held her firmly at his side, so that she could not turn. "Do not look back, sweetheart. Not when the whole world lies before us."

"Benedict." She looked up into his face. "Will *you* never look back, with regret for all you have sacrificed?"

"To Monksfield?" He shook his head. "No, love, never! When I first returned there it was a challenge to me, to see if I could make myself the next master of it, but once the prize was won, I would have wearied of it in a twelve-month. That is not the life for me. Nor, I think, is England the land for me, at least as long as the present rule holds sway."

Anxiously, her gaze searched his face. She believed that he was right, but still wished that he could have reached the decision of his own free will, without being forced to it by circumstances.

"Yet it cannot be denied," she said with a sigh, "that you are departing from England a fugitive, and in worse case than when you came home, while if it were not for me . . ."

"If it were not for you," he began, and then paused, seeking for words to tell her all that she meant to him. A purpose and a meaning to life, a renewal of faith, a deeper knowledge of himself—all these she had given him. He wanted to tell her so, to beg her forgiveness, and for a chance to make amends to her for the past, but what words were there to describe these things of which he was himself aware only instinctively, with an inner certainty which he could not express?

Her face was still upturned to his. The high cheekbones and pointed chin, the wide, sweet mouth and those strange, green eyes beneath the upward-winging brows. The face which would always hold for

221

him a quality which was more than mortal. The face of his enchantress, his elf-queen.

"Bronwen, I love you," he said simply, and knew suddenly that in those four words he had told her everything he wanted to say, or she to know.

ALL AT $1.75!

Enduring romances that represent a rich reading experience.

BABE by Joan Smith	50023
THE ELSINGHAM PORTRAIT by Elizabeth Chater	50018
FRANKLIN'S FOLLY by Georgina Grey	50026
THE HIGHLAND BROOCH by Rebecca Danton	50022
A LADY OF FORTUNE by Blanche Chenier	50028
LADY HATHAWAY'S HOUSE PARTY by Jennie Gallant	50020
THE LORD AND THE GYPSY by Patricia Veryan	50024
THE LYDEARD BEAUTY by Audrey Blanshard	50016
THE MATCHMAKERS by Rebecca Baldwin	50017
A MISTRESS TO THE REGENT by Helen Tucker	50027
REGENCY GOLD by Marion Chesney	50002
WAGER FOR LOVE by Rachelle Edwards	50012

Buy them at your local bookstore or use this handy coupon for ordering.

COLUMBIA BOOK SERVICE (a CBS Publications Co.)
32275 Mally Road, P.O. Box FB, Madison Heights, MI 48071

Please send me the books I have checked above. Orders for less than 5 books must include 75¢ for the first book and 25¢ for each additional book to cover postage and handling. Orders for 5 books or more postage is FREE. Send check or money order only.

Cost $_____   Name _____

Postage_____   Address _____

Sales tax*_____   City _____

Total $_____   State _____ Zip _____

*The government requires us to collect sales tax in all states except AK, DE, MT, NH and OR.

This offer expires 1/31/81   8000-4

MASTER NOVELISTS

CHESAPEAKE CB 24163 $3.95
by James A. Michener

An enthralling historical saga. It gives the account of different generations and races of American families who struggled, invented, endured and triumphed on Maryland's Chesapeake Bay. It is the first work of fiction in ten years to be first on *The New York Times Best Seller List*.

THE BEST PLACE TO BE PB 04024 $2.50
by Helen Van Slyke

Sheila Callaghan's husband suddenly died, her children are grown, independent and troubled, the men she meets expect an easy kind of woman. Is there a place of comfort? a place for strength against an aching void? A novel for every woman who has ever loved.

ONE FEARFUL YELLOW EYE GB 14146 $1.95
by John D. MacDonald

Dr. Fortner Geis relinquishes $600,000 to someone that no one knows. Who knows his reasons? There is a history of threats which Travis McGee exposes. But why does the full explanation live behind the eerie yellow eye of a mutilated corpse?

8002

Buy them at your local bookstore or use this handy coupon for ordering.

COLUMBIA BOOK SERVICE (a CBS Publications Co.)
32275 Mally Road, P.O. Box FB, Madison Heights, MI 48071

Please send me the books I have checked above. Orders for less than 5 books must include 75¢ for the first book and 25¢ for each additional book to cover postage and handling. Orders for 5 books or more postage is FREE. Send check or money order only.

Cost $_____ Name_____
Postage_____ Address_____
Sales tax*_____ City_____
Total $_____ State_____ Zip_____

*The government requires us to collect sales tax in all states except AK, DE, MT, NH and OR.

This offer expires 9/30/80